W9-CZX-464

ETCHED IN STONE

Dimitri Eann

The sale of this book without its cover is unauthorized. If you purchased this book without a cover, you should be aware that it was reported to the publisher as "unsold and destroyed." Neither the author nor the publisher has received payment for the sale of this "stripped book."

ETCHED IN STONE

Published by ImaJinn Books, a division of ImaJinn

Copyright ©2000 by Dimitri Fitchett

Printed and bound in the United States of America. All rights reserved. No part of this book may be reproduced in any form or by any means (electronic, mechanical, photocopying, recording, or otherwise) without prior written permission of both the copyright holder and the above publisher of this book, except by a reviewer, who may quote brief passages in a review. For information, address: ImaJinn Books, a division of ImaJinn, P.O. Box 162, Hickory Corners, MI 49060-0162; or call toll free 1-877-625-3592.

First Printing June, 2000

ISBN: 1-893896-12-9

PUBLISHER'S NOTE:
This book is a work of fiction. Names, characters, places and incidents are products of the author's imagination or are used fictitiously. Any resemblance to actual events or locales or persons, living or dead, is entirely coincidental.

Books are available at quantity discounts when used to promote products or services. For information please write to: Marketing Division, ImaJinn Books, P.O. Box 162, Hickory Corners, MI 49060-0162, or call toll free 1-877-625-3592.

Cover design by Patricia Lazarus

ImaJinn Books, a division of ImaJinn
P.O. Box 162, Hickory Corners, MI 49060-0162
Toll Free: 1-877-625-3592
http://www.imajinnbooks.com

DEDICATION

To Mike—for your support and encouragement.
To Aleigha—for your everything.
To Michael—for the high-fives.
To Jillayne—for the photography,
And to Gwen—for asking if we're going to dance in the kitchen again.

A special thank you and deepest appreciation to Linda Kichline. Thank you, Linda!

Note from ImaJinn Books

Dear Readers,

Thank you for buying this book. The author has worked hard to bring you a captivating tale of love and adventure.

In the months ahead, watch for our fast-paced, action-packed stories involving ghosts, psychics and psychic phenomena, witches, vampires, werewolves, angels, reincarnation, futuristic in space or on other planets, futuristic on earth, time travel to the past, time travel to the present, and any other story line that will fall into the "New-Age" category.

The best way for us to give you the types of books you want to read is to hear from you. Let us know your favorite types of "New-Age" romance. You may write to us or any of our authors at: ImaJinn Books, P.O. Box 162, Hickory Corners, MI 49060-0162. You may also e-mail us at imajinn@worldnet.att.net.

Be sure to visit our web site at:
http://www.imajinnbooks.com

CHAPTER ONE

Deep in the heart of Egypt, low in the bowels of an ancient tomb, twenty-two-year-old Boston University graduate Jayna Monroe lay gasping her last breaths. No one had set foot inside the tomb in over four thousand years—not robbers, not explorers. No one had looked upon, or touched its bounty until Jayna stumbled upon its hidden door, sheltered by a sand dune beneath a low cliff.

Her party of Egyptologists were digging too far away. She'd sensed it and gone exploring on her own, three nights before, with nothing more than a torch. That very torch told her how much time had passed while she'd sought her way back out. She'd lost the entrance and had searched, at first calmly, then frantically, then hysterically. The flame on the three-day torch was almost out.

The water in her body was, also, almost out. She lay on the cold floor, the packed earth working its chill through her bones, but she couldn't bring herself to get up. She was done with searching the tunnels and passageways of the man she'd deciphered to be the Great King Amony. Her amazement at the beauty of the hieroglyphs—the words, the artwork, the treasures of gold and jewels—had long since faded. A few hours ago, before the last of her energy was spent, she'd crawled out of the king's burial chamber and into this small, dank-smelling antechamber, desperate to find some secret passage to the outside that she hadn't discovered before. Now, believing with all her heart that she was going to die, Jayna wished she had the strength to go back to the king. Four thousand years or four minutes, death was death, and she didn't want to die alone.

But she couldn't move.

Hieroglyphs surrounded her, words and pictures she'd paid little attention to when she'd been searching for the way out of the tomb. Now she could do nothing but look at them, and she let the panic in her mind dwindle with her failing body. She wouldn't think of the search party that would never find her in time. She wouldn't think of death, of the life she was leaving behind forever. Her throat tightened. She wouldn't think of her parents, professors both, adopting her as a baby and raising her as their own child, giving her birthday parties and hugs, leading her into their love of Egyptology. She hadn't been able, as she'd hoped, to give her parents grandchildren before they passed away, but she'd comforted herself with the knowledge that she'd been both child and grandchild to the aged couple.

The worst thought in all this was what she'd never get to do in life. She'd never have babies of her own. She'd never fall in love.

How fitting that she should die here—she who'd been abandoned at birth on the front walk of the Administration Building at Boston University. No one knew where she had come from. Now, no one would know where she'd gone. She had to wonder if anyone would care.

A dry, guttural moan came from deep in her throat, and her heart spasmed. *Think something else, Jayna, think anything else.*

She looked to the hieroglyphs on the wall. A queen, she deciphered quickly. King Amony's queen. A beautiful, green-eyed woman....

Jayna's dry throat tightened around a painful lump. So, the eternal happiness of the man to whom this entire tomb and its enclosed fortune was dedicated had been married and left behind a wife to mourn his passing. He hadn't been alone, like her. If the hereafter ran the way the ancient Egyptians believed, her body, enclosed in this tomb, would make her entire twenty-two years of existence no different from the solid gold staff in the burial chamber, or the jar of incense in the passageway—just a token treasure for the Great King Amony's afterlife enjoyment.

The writing on the wall started to blur. Jayna closed her eyes a moment, then opened them and deciphered some more.

Queen—no name for the woman—the Queen was wicked, a traitor to the throne. She'd devised many plots, had many failures, but finally one traitorous plan had worked. The Queen's own hand had carried out her only success. She'd killed her husband.

Jayna turned her head, her dark hair trailing across the floor as she gazed toward the burial chamber. The King's life, and passing out of that life, seemed suddenly as lonely as hers. His own wife had killed him—not accident, nor disease, nor foolish curiosity—his wife had killed him.

She closed her eyes. She was so tired.

Amony. She forced her brain to function. He'd been a fairly young man, not much older than her twenty-two years, according to the images on the walls. And he was handsome, judging by the drawings and statues and exquisite burial mask made of him. What could have possessed the queen to kill her own husband? Had she been wicked, or had he been a cruel, violent man?

The questions in her mind tired her, warning her: Stay awake! Stay alert! Her bottom lip trembled, and her eyes burned for lack of tears. She drew a deep breath, only too aware how feeble the effort was.

Anyone who could rule an entire country had to be strong, she thought in desperation, holding onto life with the power of her mind. Had the king been vicious? Abusive?

She looked back to the hieroglyphs. *Keep thinking, keep living.*

There was only more condemnation of the queen, accompanied by pictures of the royal couple's daily life—attending court, each seated upon their gilded chairs; at an ostrich hunt; standing beside the River Nile. No picture showed the queen's hands. They were always portrayed as deviously hidden behind her back. Finally, there was the picture of the killing, blood dripping from the queen's fingertips, her husband's face anguished and surprised.

It was too much—the violence of so many years ago, the effort of concentrating, of keeping her eyes open. The effort of breathing.

The king. She forced her mind away from the helpless, terrifying truth of her situation and thought of the king lying in the dark chamber next to her. She tried to open her eyes. She wanted just one more look. She had to see him, his casket. She was losing her mind, surely, as assuredly as she was losing her life, but she didn't want to be alone. She wanted to see another who'd crossed that barrier she was about to experience. She needed comfort.

The foot of his casket gleamed a duller black in her ever-darkening vision. With a loneliness and despair she knew he must have felt in those final moments of his life, her failing heart cried out to him. Amony...Amony...

"Amony!" His name tore through her chest and past her lips.

All went still.

Like the silence after the snapping of a twig, quiet descended. Her pain vanished—her physical pain, for her heartache and loss still hovered over her, a separate entity, not bound by time or place or circumstance. Yet she was apart from it, looking at it with eyes that couldn't see and a heart that shouldn't feel. Her soul floated above her, dark and black and as lonely as King Amony's casket gleaming in the centuries-old tomb.

She was in a void of nothingness — floating, detached. How long she remained that way, she didn't know, but she knew when it ended. She felt it, somehow, when it slammed against her: the pressure—first and foremost on her numbed chest and through to her back. It bored through her, and around her, spinning her, sucking at her, swinging her arms and legs wide from her torso. She was falling. Or soaring. Blackness swirling around her. She, spiraling through a darkness so great that she thought to be lost, finally and at last, the insignificant being that she was...

'But I'm someone!' Her spirit cried for her. 'I'm someone!'

'I'm someone. I'm someone...' it echoed.

As abruptly as it had left her, it returned: the black fog of anguish and despair that colored King Amony's tomb.

Her spirit rushed into her.

The ground met her back.

"Your Highness. Wake up." Low, urgent words. "Wake up, Your Highness."

Oxygen hit Jayna's lungs, and she drew it in with a gasp that felt sure to explode her chest. Her eyes opened. The sun blinded her from high overhead, its brilliance stunning her dilated pupils. Heat sweltered from above and around her. Encroaching palm trees encircled her and cast their shade, only half-heartedly reducing the temperature in the little glade. A brightly-colored blanket lay beneath her bare calves and arms. Five or six women sat several yards away, crowded around a board-game, and a dark-haired, dark-eyed man hovered over her, speaking to her. And she could hear him.

She was alive! Yes. Air rushed through her lungs. Her heart thumped against her breastbone—a sluggish thumping, though it was, for the heat that surrounded her. She sat up quickly.

"Calm yourself," the man whispered. "You'll give us away. And for the lives of more than you care to count, wipe that look from your face. Your husband's followers will remember theatrics such as this."

"Wha—" Jayna couldn't get her tongue to work.

Of course her tongue didn't work. She wasn't alive, after all; she was dead, or dreaming, or hallucinating. More pertinent to the moment, given the man who stared directly into her eyes, she was confused.

She thrust herself to her feet.

"What are you talking about?" Her words came out in the clear, ancient Hamitic tongue, stunning her, and she glanced down at herself. Her own tanned feet and legs peeked out, very life-like and full of energy beneath a pleated and shockingly sheer-white dress. A jeweled belt cinched her waist, and a drop of sweat trickled down under the thick, jeweled necklace that lay across her throat. Blood pulsed forcefully through every vein in her body, fueling every nerve-ending. Adrenaline pumped through her. Life rushed through her.

What? What? What?

"What does this mean?" she whispered.

"The priestesses." The man interpreted her confusion for something less than the literal life-or-death question that it was. With a glance, he turned her attention to the women who sat in the circle on the blanket, playing their game. "We can't be sure of the loyalty of each and every one of them. Our helpers are in place and Amony awaits us."

Amony.

Jayna took a step back.

"Are you up to it?" he asked. "I fear you're not up to it. It's just to the break between the trees." In a louder voice, he asked, "A walk, my Queen?" A few of the women glanced over at them. Softer, for Jayna's ears only, he said, "A few small steps. Your ladies won't think a thing." He stepped aside, allowing her space to pass him.

Jayna hesitated. How could this be happening? Had she died and followed the Great King Amony into his afterlife? Was there some power in the majestic, mysterious tomb that could transport her into his presence? Had the Egyptians been right all along about preserving themselves and their worldly treasures that they might live again and make use of their riches?

It was an incredible thought, but the Egyptologist in her was ready to believe it. The twenty-first century woman that she was, however, found one serious flaw in her predicament. Why had she, however temporarily, been thrust into the role of queen—a killer-queen, of all people? She'd no sooner harm a fly than a man, and she certainly had no illusions that royal blood ran in her veins. She was a cast-off at birth, for goodness' sake.

Not to mention the fact that her eyes were brown, not green. The hieroglyphs had been specific about that detail concerning the woman. Didn't this man notice the difference? She glanced down at her toes. They were definitely her toes. Surely her eyes were their usual brown.

One thing was certain. She had to go to Amony. He was waiting. Did Amony have something to say to her? She'd very much like to see the man who lay near her in death and hear the words he might speak.

Taking a step forward, she looked to the women who appeared unconcerned with her movement. She wandered with her escort to the break in the trees, and stepped into the impossibly hotter air of the Egyptian countryside.

A hint of recognition stopped her. This was it. The place. Four thousand years from now this glade would be but a spattering of struggling branches. She knew, because it was where her party had set up camp. And the dunes that had beckoned to her in the distance that fatal night were none other than what lay before her now as she turned and looked down into a shallow valley: the coverings of the tomb of the Great King Amony.

She stared out at the thousands of men who labored, pushing bricks she knew to weigh at least a ton, over telephone pole-like logs and up a mud-made ramp. They sweated beneath the hot, Egyptian sun, erecting the building of worship and spiritual afterlife, like a scene from a picture-book, but moving with true vigor, true life.

How could this all be so clear? Was she being granted a vision of what she'd only glimpsed as an Egyptologist, an insight into what she'd made her entire life? Was a Greater Being allowing her this last moment of beauty before oblivion—before hell—before heaven—

Am I in heaven? She felt as though she were in heaven as she looked down on the laborers. Even from this distance she could see the differences in their faces—the character, reflecting the trials of each man's life. No drawings could capture this, no drawings had quite succeeded, either, but she was seeing it first-hand, of that she had no doubt.

"I'm alive," she breathed. "I'm really alive."

The man's hand slid into hers. "I know what you mean." His eyes danced with wild lights, then his face turned in profile to her as he gazed into the valley. "The world will never forget this day, because of us. There he is. The Pharaoh. Your husband."

Jayna looked back to the valley. Her gaze caught on a dash of blue upon the head of a man near the bottom of the ramp. The color told her all. The workers' heads were shaven, their garments a simple white that began at their waists and ended above the knee. This man, by contrast, wore a pale-blue head-covering that drew down to flaps ending below his shoulders. A broad circlet of color encased his throat—reminiscent of Jayna's own necklace—and gold bands glinted from both his upper arms and his ankles. Wide, tanned biceps crossed authoritatively over a thick chest, and sturdy legs spread shoulder-length apart, supporting a slim torso. She was gazing upon Amony. King Amony. Pharaoh. Husband. Unexpected pride stiffened her backbone. She felt taller, suddenly—straighter, stronger. She felt, incredibly, like a queen married to a king.

"Spit on him. Spit now, while the brick still holds and he yet has life."

Spit? Jayna turned to her companion in disbelief. Spit?

Our helpers are in place, he'd said, *and Amony awaits us. Are you up to it? I fear you're not up to it.*

Jayna felt as though all the blood drained from her body in one great rush. Was this a plot to kill King Amony? If this was an assassination attempt, she wasn't up to it. She definitely wasn't up to it. Lying in his tomb, she'd felt for the man; why should she have to watch him die?

To not feel so alone—the answer came to her. Though she'd felt the king's presence from the other room—from the other side of four thousand years—she'd been alone, and she didn't want to be.

But why, why should she have to witness this event? Because he was witness to her death?

Ba. Ka. Did his spirit forms really still roam the tomb, watching, punishing her for her entrance into his sanctuary, punishing her for having to witness her agony as she gave up her life, as surely as she trembled at the thought of watching this proud man fall beneath the tumble of brick?

"No," the denial rushed from her. Her own death was hard enough to accept without watching another's pain. It eased her suffering not a bit.

The hieroglyphs. The word-pictures had said Amony died by his wife's own hand. The queen had devised many plots, which failed, forcing her to kill him personally. It hadn't been a vague conceptualization. The queen had done it herself, with her own hands.

Jayna clenched her fists into tight balls and nodded as her fingernails bit into her palms. They hurt her. She felt pain. And she knew who she was.

At this moment, King Amony's queen was standing at the top of a hill, wearing a far-too-see-through dress—and she was only part of a plot. Amony might have died with a single knife blade in his back, but he most certainly hadn't died under the crushing weight of one of the ton-heavy bricks from his own tomb. Relief tore through her, but her voice shook as she turned to the man. "It won't work. The plan is wrong. It won't work."

He didn't look at her. She heard a snap, and shouts, and followed the direction of his greedy gaze. The entire crew on the lowest part of the ramp leaped aside as the brick they handled disengaged and slid backward, straight toward their pharaoh. Seconds later King Amony was swallowed by an enormous red cloud of dust and debris.

"No," Jayna breathed. "No." She said it again, louder. "No, it's not right! It's not right!"

She didn't realize she had backed away, retreating into the glade, until her women rushed up and surrounded her, murmuring, plying her with questions.

"What is it, Your Highness?"

"She's as pale as death."

"What's wrong? What happened?"

He—the crazed one, the killer, the plotter—hurried to them. Jayna shrank back.

"It's the Pharaoh." His chest rose and fell dramatically as he panted out the words. False innocence and an even falser concern darkened his eyes. "There's been an accident in the valley. We saw the brick fall."

Gasps emitted from the group. One woman gave a cry of anguish and ran to the break in the trees that Jayna had just vacated. An older woman followed, cradled the younger, trying to calm her—to hush her, Jayna thought, when the woman's worried gaze shot her way. This would be the Queen's moment, evidently, but Jayna didn't begrudge the other her grief. Anyone with an ounce of compassion would be moved by the knowledge that a man might have just lost his life.

The elder of the group, a woman of some forty years, with a profusion of jewels on every extremity, put her arm around Jayna's shoulders and addressed the man. "Go, Hareb. Find out if he lives. The Queen needs comfort."

"Yes, go," the other women agreed. "Tiy's right. He may still live. Go find out."

The man named Hareb hurried away, and the woman called Tiy pulled Jayna out of the group. "The rest of you, watch from the break and see if you can bring us some word."

Jayna allowed the woman to walk her away. She didn't want to see any bodies pulled out from the debris, bodies that she, in this role of queen, would have to claim partial responsibility for. Already her chest tightened, her stomach churned, at this unthinkable matter of murder.

Tiy patted her shoulder. "We'll come out of this just fine, either way. Don't worry."

A small, secret smile lay beneath her words, and Jayna stopped. She knew, at once, that the woman was one of them—a conspirator to King Amony's killing. Tiy's arm slid off Jayna's shoulders, for which Jayna was glad. The woman's touch repulsed her.

"He lives!"

The cry came from behind them, and Jayna spun around.

The women waved excitedly. "He's alive. Come see. He's up and walking!"

Tiy gripped Jayna's arm, pulling her close. "We must think." She paused a moment, then called to the women, "We'll return to the palace, then, to greet him. The Queen needs time to compose herself. Stay and watch. Just be along to prepare for the feast."

Knowing nods abounded. The woman who'd first rushed to the break sobbed quietly, but she managed a slight bow, along with the others, as Tiy pulled Jayna past them.

The temperature seemed to rise thirty degrees as they stepped out of the glade and headed across the sand to a building that shimmered in the distance. Jayna already felt light-headed, out-of-control, on the verge of seeing a mirage. Surely the building they approached was merely that, a figment of her ever-broadening imagination: a beautiful palace of whitewashed mud-brick, and terraces, trimmed with palm trees that shaded a gleaming blue pool of cool water.

Tiy spoke, turning her beautiful mirage into a nightmare. "The first foray didn't do the deed, but we'll try again. Accidents. Accidents are the best approach. An unlucky pharaoh. Better yet, a pharaoh so frowned upon from the heavens that his destruction has been sought. The people will long remember the unfavored one. We'll do it. Just keep your wits about you and play the game. More lives than yours are forfeit if this is found out."

Jayna looked at the woman as they plodded through the sand. Heat nudged up through her sandals, and she felt sweat pop everywhere on her body, even through the backs of her hands. The words that echoed in her ears, of killing and collaboration, brought a scowl to her lips. Her nostrils flared as she gritted her teeth. "I don't regard this as a game."

Tiy took the statement in stride, and with pleasure, for she smiled. "And thus the reason you were chosen for this marriage. You are very strong, as strong as I, but getting the Pharaoh to wed this face of mine would have been impossible." She laughed with delight, as if the man she spoke of wasn't the man she hoped to murder. "Nothing will come of our plans, however, if we let this first failure eat at us. Ho—they made great speed."

A clamor of voices and running feet rose to the left, near the palace grounds, to greet the arrival. So many people rushed from the doors and down through the gates that Jayna wondered if word of Amony's accident inspired this greeting, or if it was normal procedure. The former seemed the case as chariot after chariot raced forward from the west and stopped on the edges of the throng. The original chariot sat idle. Its noble personage met the crowd on foot.

"It's him?" Jayna asked, craning her neck for a glimpse of the king. "It's Amony?"

Tiy looked at her in surprise, then laughed. "Save your innocence for him. He can't suspect a thing."

Then Jayna saw him—a glimpse of the pale-blue linen head-covering, struck through with alternate lines of white that hadn't been visible from the earlier distance, above a sturdy, supple, red-brown chest. The crowd was thick, affording her little view, but here he was, King Amony in his heyday, walking among his people. Excitement rose, tightening the back of her throat. It's him! It's him! She hurried forward to get a better glimpse. He was still some fifty yards, and as many heads, away when he looked to his right, allowing her a full, frontal view of him.

She smiled.

He was handsome—handsome beyond the evidence of his tomb. The artists who'd turned their hands to Amony's countenance hadn't been flatterers, but realists. Realists, yet humans, she thought as her hungry gaze drank in his high-cheekbones and strong, rectangular face. Only so much could be done with stone and with gold. Only so much could be done with paint. Art couldn't capture the essence of the man, and this man, in particular—powerful, vital, and infinitely beautiful—had eluded art.

Jayna moved forward, determined to see him closer still. The people who blocked her shifted and moved aside as she worked her way steadily onward. She paused at a break that allowed her another clear look, and watched in awe as he passed through the crowd. His gaze moved with leisure over the various people. They were absorbing, deep-brown eyes set above a full-lipped mouth that stretched in a natural, comfortable smile. Amony was at ease with himself and his flock.

Jayna edged nearer. She was no more than twenty yards away when his expression changed suddenly, and for no apparent reason. She started to glance away, to find the source of his—displeasure, was it? His smile had faded, and he looked almost as if he were bracing himself. Then his gaze lifted and his eyes met hers.

Jayna's breath left her chest, and her legs turned to air beneath her. Her skin tingled, almost a reminder to her stalled heart, for it leapt back into action a moment later, thudding harder and heavier with every passing second that their gazes held. They might have been back in the tomb again, just her and Amony, one on one, intimate and alone.

He knew her. He knew....

The dark, compelling gaze didn't leave her as he bent his head to the side and spoke to the man nearest him. The fellow—his black hair cropped short—nodded, then detached himself and shoved through the crowd, heading directly for her.

Amony finally turned away.

Jayna drew in a deep, much-needed breath.

Twining her fingers tightly together, she fought to clamp down her anticipation as the courtier neared.

The man stopped before her and bowed low. "Your Highness. The Great Pharaoh Amony sends word that he wishes to receive you in his private chambers."

Chapter Two

The crowd had fallen back, forming a large circle in which she stood center. Jayna managed a nod for the man, then a tight vise seized her arm. Before she could draw another breath, Tiy pulled her away through the throng that parted quickly, reverent now, at seeing who needed admittance.

Private chambers, the words echoed through Jayna's mind. Amony wanted to meet with her in his private chambers. Looking into his eyes in the company of a hundred other people was one thing, but meeting in his private chambers?

She stumbled in the thick, loose sand. "Tiy." She swallowed heavily. "I'm not doing very well."

The lines between the woman's dark eyes burrowed deeper. "You have to do this." She glanced around, then steered them off the path they were traveling, away from the mainstream of traffic. "We'll go in through the pool doors."

Jayna nodded as if it were the most natural of ideas.

They fought the sand a few minutes longer, then Tiy twined her arm with Jayna's and reassured her. "The Pharaoh has no way of knowing you had anything to do with the rope snapping."

Jayna lurched to a standstill. A bucket of cold water thrown into her face couldn't have sobered her more. Her worry, to this point, lay in the thought of coming face-to-face with Amony, a twenty-first century woman meeting an ancient king.

Her situation was far worse than that. She was also a wife—that king's wife. The woman who sought his death. The realization set her nerves twisting all the tighter. Denial swept through her.

"But did I know about the rope snapping? Did I know?"

"No, Your Highness." Tiy raised her hands in a show of innocence, but the tone of her voice proved it a flat, obvious lie. "You didn't know. How could you have known such a thing would happen?"

Jayna twisted past the woman, stifling a moan as she trudged on through the sand. She'd known all about it. She'd gone along with it. How? How could she be so cold-blooded? How could she enter the body of anyone so calculating and murderous?

She glanced at her feet again, then at the backs of her hands, her forearms, her palms. The realization struck, once more, that she appeared to be inhabiting her own body.

Okay. She moistened dry lips. This is my body, but not my role. But I'm in this role. Why? Am I supposed to warn him? *'Your Highness, I'm going to try to kill you, but don't take it out on me just now. I'm not myself today.'*

They reached the base of the stairs where two stiff-faced guards stood at attention, massive arms crossed over broad, bare chests. Jayna hesitated and Tiy took the lead, drawing her past them and up the steps. At the top, opening off a wall of curved archways and thick pillars, lay a plush terrace. Plump, white lotus blooms floated on the surface of a large pool. Palm trees cast their shade on reed-hewn lounge chairs and small tables with flowery centerpieces.

A tingle of alarm ran through Jayna, raising the soft hairs on her arms. Why had she gone to the glade when this spot was available?

Boredom, she thought. *Monotony*. The glade was pleasant and different. That it overlooked the valley of her husband's tomb, and she went there today, the very day of his accident, was only coincidence.

Stepping with Tiy through the archway of the palace, Jayna felt almost blinded. The bright sun had played havoc with her eyes, and she couldn't see where she was going in the dimmer interior. Tiy seemed to have less difficulty—she drew Jayna on without missing a step. Jayna blinked furiously to clear her eyes. She couldn't miss this, the only genuine view any Egyptologist had ever had of an ancient palace in action.

The corridor was enormous, tall and broad, with strange, part-animal/part-man likenesses of various gods painted upon the walls. Statues of the same, inlaid with colored stones, stood stiff and splendid every few feet. A large man, identical to the guards they'd encountered outside the terrace steps, attended a door several feet ahead.

Tiy slowed just short of that portal. Amony's chamber? Jayna hadn't time to relish the antiquities. She had a king to face. A king she—or rather the woman she inhabited—was trying to kill.

She whirled to Tiy. "I don't know what to say to him."

Tiy gripped her shoulders. "Take advantage of the trauma of the day. You're distraught. Stunned. This will explain your lack of words. And tears."

She took her arm and led Jayna past the guard and through the door, into an elaborate reception room. Straight ahead stood another guard and another door. "Go," Tiy urged. "He'll be pleased enough that you cared to come."

'Cared to come?' Jayna felt quite 'forced to come' as she stepped hesitantly toward the door and the guard. Knowing herself to be a trespasser, she quailed inwardly, but the man didn't bat an eyelash as she moved past him and into the Pharaoh's chamber.

The door shut behind her. The room, no less than thirty-feet-square, was fit for a king. Intricately painted tiles lined the floor. A curator's dream adorned the walls and twisted along the legs of chairs and chests in the forms of Isis and Osiris, carvings of lion's paws and panther skin—gold and ebony. Mats, woven in brilliant blue, green, and red, lay strategically about the floor—a centerpiece to the sitting-room style of this nearer part of the chamber, and a welcome to the feet at both sides of the enormous bed that dominated the far wall.

Jayna glanced between the two closed doors that stood about midway on each side of the room. As she stepped forward and satisfied her almost overwhelming need to touch the treasures of the room, she hoped they would stay closed a while longer. Such beauty in its natural setting could only be imagined when one saw the individual pieces tagged and stacked for museum display.

Caressing the sleek, dark wood of one chair's arm, she drifted farther, and drew her fingers over the smooth surface of a low table. Her gaze moved to the carved inlay at the footboard of the bed, and she ambled near, a cautious eye on all of the doors.

King Amony's bed, she thought with awe.

Heavy, artfully-turned wood encased the structure. Carefully stacked cushions served as a mattress and underlay the sparkling golden sheet. Pillows of gold, yellow, and blue reclined alongside each other like dominoes against the equally ornate headboard.

King Amony's bed, she marveled again. His place of rest, for a night, for a few hours. She couldn't help visualizing that other place, the chamber of his eternal rest, and she shuddered.

Reaching out, she touched the gold linen. Softness met her fingertips. Softness and warmth. Pleasure tip-toed through her. He was alive. For this moment, this day, the man rested here, in comfort and warmth. He'd sleep here tonight, and he'd see the sun rise on the morrow.

A faint footstep sounded from beyond the door on her left, startling her. Her gentle thoughts fled before a tide of panic. What would she say to him?

She hurried back to the portal where Tiy had left her and took up position just beside it.

The distant door swung open, and the Pharaoh stepped through. Thick muscle stretched beneath taut, tan skin, anklets and bracelets flashed—and power filled the room.

He didn't acknowledge her. He didn't glance her way. She went unnoticed as he raised a thick arm and pulled the headdress from black hair that tapered away from his temples and brushed near his nape.

Silk, shot through with blue fire.

This was the man the Queen wanted dead?

The dark head bowed, and the sculpted torso curved inward as Amony leaned his back against the wall.

Something's wrong, Jayna thought. Something serious. Her heart fluttered near her throat. *The brick... Does he know?*

His face raised slowly, and he looked at her. Deep-brown, near-black eyes gazed into her soul. He spoke, his voice low, and deep, and slightly breathless. "You're here."

An aura of strength, a might beyond the raw, visual impact inspired by his virile body, radiated from him with a force that stunned Jayna's senses. The chamber seemed to shrink and narrow with his potent presence. The room wasn't large enough—indeed, the far reaches of time itself hadn't sufficed to leave her unmoved by his power.

Jayna opened her mouth, but no words would come.

The headdress slipped from Amony's fingers and fell to the floor. He pushed away from the wall with the slow, steady movements of a lion awakening in the sun, and a new wave of panic washed through her. Her frightened gaze locked on his dark, determined eyes as he stepped toward her. The distance between them shortened. The heat of his body mixed with the growing warmth of hers. She shrank back against the wall.

His right arm raised, and he leaned toward her, settling his forearm on the wall near her face. She was trapped and didn't dare breathe for fear the slightest movement of her chest would bring her in contact with his bare flesh.

To her disbelief, she saw that small, faint freckles dotted the reddish-hued skin of his slim nose and high cheekbones. Just when his power most overwhelmed her, this sight, so incredibly youthful, and normal, and endearing, served to completely unnerve her. Nothing in the tomb had even hinted of this. 'The man is a god,' it had fairly screamed. Not, 'the god is a man.' It wasn't fair. She wasn't prepared—

His dark gaze moved over her face and delved into her eyes. "I'm alive."

The soft utterance shuddered through her senses, but before she could gather her fleeting wits, his head dipped near hers. The firm muscle of his chest met her racing heart, and that silken hair brushed against her neck—

The pressure of his head alongside hers intensified. The weight of his chest became suddenly heavier. His taut body went still. Gravity was taking over and he was doing nothing to stop it. He'd lost consciousness!

With a gasp, Jayna threw her arms around his waist. She cradled his large body against hers, her hands straining against the rock-hard flesh of his back.

Yet, as swiftly as he'd sagged, he straightened, jerking upright from the certain fall. He steadied himself with his left hand against the wall, and the forearm that had slipped for that single moment reclaimed its position.

Jayna withdrew her arms carefully from his bare, heated flesh, and her heart beat a new tempo that set her limbs shaking. He was hurt. He'd been injured, after all. She had to get help for him, but how did one tell a king to remove his arms and step away?

His eyes were glazed as he looked at her. He blinked to clear them, and only half succeeded. They remained an unfocused, faded brown.

"I'm alive," he said again, as if the past few seconds had never occurred. She sensed that, to him, they hadn't.

"I'm very glad—"

"I see your gladness." He cut through her unnerved comment, denying her the opportunity to follow it up with her concern for his health. "Hareb claimed you—" He winced and clenched his teeth.

Seeing her opening, Jayna started to speak, but a thunderous pounding shook the door beside them. "Your Highness, Atep is here. I've brought the healer."

A doctor! Jayna nodded, relieved.

Amony ignored the intrusion. The skin stretched tighter over his tanned face, but he recovered from whatever pain had seized him, and continued on. "Hareb claimed—you were near hysteria."

"Your Highness." A heavy fist beat on the door again. "I beg you answer. The healer is here."

Amony's darkening gaze didn't falter. Jayna glanced past his large bicep to the door. Obviously, the King would have his say.

"I—I saw the brick fall," she said.

"You've collected yourself."

It was an observation, not a question.

"Your Highness—!" Thunder sounded against the wood.

Thunder beside her, lightning in front of her. She knew which to heed.

Amony suggested that she'd collected herself. She shook her head. "Only partially."

A voice called beyond the door. "You must answer, Your Highness. We'll wait if you require it, but we need to hear from you."

Amony stared into her eyes for a long moment, then he smiled, a joyless smile that drew his mouth into a tight line. Had her answer not pleased him? Shifting his weight, he withdrew his left arm, opening her path to the door. A great weariness filled his voice. "Now that our—emotional display—is over, I'd like to admit the public."

Jayna looked at the door, then back to him.

His eyelids dipped, then raised slowly. He was having difficulty focusing again. His darkened eyes were reversing to the faded brown. "You may leave, Jayna."

Jayna? He'd called her Jayna!

The meeting was far from complete, but the man needed medical help. She had to go if it meant letting the doctor in. She turned and opened the door. A full six men crowded without. She flattened herself against the doorframe as they raced in past her, and past Amony. Sandaled feet stalled, heads turned, gazes searching for the Pharaoh in the huge chamber.

Jayna raised a hand to direct them, then gasped as Amony crumpled toward the floor. She lunged forward. Two pairs of strong arms reached him first. She stepped back as the others shouldered their way to the king's body. Stretching out his long frame—he was at least two or three inches over six feet tall—the men lifted him and carried him across the room to the bed. Jayna followed the frightening procession, a careful eye on the Pharaoh's pallid face, and took up vigil at the ornately-carved footboard.

The healer placed a cloth bag on the bedside, and urged the men who lined up alongside him, "Remove his clothes."

Jayna hesitated at the order and stepped back a pace. She watched the physician. Would he know what to do with Amony, or was the king's injury to be one of those beyond the medical capability of the day? The ancient Egyptians had been quite adept at medicine, but this was Amony. Nothing could go wrong. He had to survive.

The low exclamations as Amony's kilt was pulled back drew her gaze to the dark, purple bruise covering his right hip. She pressed her fingertips to her mouth.

The healer crouched over the contusion, blocking her view. "And he walked up here from the yard?"

Jayna's thoughts echoed his dismayed question. No wonder he'd kept resting against the walls!

Atep's ministrations brought a groan from the king.

He was regaining consciousness. His eyelids fluttered open. He turned his head on the pillow and scanned the faces around him. His gaze touched her a moment, then rolled to the men. "Remove the Queen."

Jayna. Queen. He believed she was his wife.

Clamping her fingers together, Jayna took a step forward. "I should stay." She didn't want to leave the chamber until she knew he was going to be all right. "You're hurt. I should stay."

He appeared to consider her words, then a grimace of pain tore across his features. Whatever torture he endured subsided only slightly before he rasped again, "Remove the Queen."

A tall, stiff-faced man stepped away from the side of the bed and came around to her. Jayna stole one more glance at Amony, then turned reluctantly and fell in step with the man.

"He's in a great deal of pain."

She looked up into surprisingly kind eyes. When the man had come for her, she'd expected stony silence and a sneer or two. "I knew he was hurt," she said, "but I thought—maybe it was his head."

Soft laughter met her comment. "At it, even now." He put his arm around her back, surprising her, as he guided her into the reception room.

Who was this man?

They stopped before the main door and he gave her shoulders a gentle squeeze. "Don't worry. He'll pull through."

He seemed...genuine. It was a good feeling. He even believed she was concerned about her husband, a wonderful change from the other people she'd met here.

She smiled her pleasure. "Thank you."

White teeth flashed in a grin.

Jayna nodded at the man, then opened the door and stepped out into the hall. Some twenty feet past the guard, the woman, Tiy, lounged against the wall, her bracelet-bedecked arms wrapped intimately around a man's bare back. Jayna took a quick step in the other direction.

"How is he?" Tiy's voice raised to carry to her.

Jayna couldn't very well ignore the question without being obvious. Her feet drew to a hesitant stop. She didn't know where she was going, anyway.

She turned around and awaited the couple. They approached her with light steps, their arms entwined. The man was an equal to Tiy in looks, somewhat broad about the cheekbones, nearing middle-age, and a bit distinguished-looking for his maturity. Tiy's hair remained a deep black, but the man who claimed her arm had grayed prematurely, imparting to him a dignified ashen head of hair.

Hope lit both their faces.

"The healer went in," Tiy said. "He's injured, isn't he?"

The man nodded, one dark brow arched high in anticipation. As an intimate of Tiy's, he was no doubt eager for a gruesome accounting of blood and gore spilled from Amony's tender flesh.

Jayna masked her disgust, but she couldn't resist dashing their hopes. "Word has it he'll live."

The couple exchanged glances.

Tiy patted her companion's bare chest. "Go in and do your part, Sefu."

Jayna stiffened. "What do you intend?"

The man's long, imperious-looking nose raised a notch. "To play the concerned friend and noble, of course."

"Let him know I'm comforting the queen," Tiy said.

"Of course." The man patted Tiy tenderly on the cheek, and there seemed to be something of the actor about him as he said, "My bride-to-be has such love for the Pharaoh and his wife."

With a tight smile, he turned and walked back toward Amony's chamber. Tiy took Jayna's arm and steered her in the direction which Jayna had thought to flee the meeting altogether.

"How did it go?"

Several responses passed through Jayna's mind, but none she could express to this woman. "Fine," she said. "Better than I expected."

Tiy nodded. "I told you it would go well. Ugh—"

They'd rounded the corridor, and Tiy stared moodily at the large man loitering near a door on the distant right. Almost as big as the guard who stood at attention a few feet beyond him, this man was thick-bodied, yet soft-looking. Though he appeared to be nearing middle-age, he still wore the single ponytail on the side of his head that proclaimed him not yet a man. Jayna frowned. Something about the way he moved bothered her. He kept his head down, taking only furtive peeks as they approached, and his feet and legs moved constantly, as if they'd carry him fleeing in fright. Yet he went nowhere. Step forward, step back. Step sideways, step back.

"Your imbecile awaits you," Tiy drawled. "I don't know how you tolerate him. Be gone, Mamo," she ordered as they neared him. "The Queen hasn't time for you today."

The overgrown man flinched and ducked his head deeper into his chest. He started to dash away, but Jayna's heart went out to him. "No," she said. "Mamo, come back."

If Tiy didn't like this Mamo, he was bound to be a good person. Ignoring the woman's exasperated sigh, she coaxed the shy man toward her with a wave of her hand. "Come here."

He wouldn't look directly at her, but he obeyed, his tense body visibly relaxing. Like a child, he stretched out his hands—enormous, awkward hands. Not knowing what else to do, Jayna held her own out to him.

He dropped a stone-carving into her palms. She stared at the figurine in surprise, then drew it to her for closer examination. It was Hathor, goddess of love and the protector of women, carved to the finest detail.

"Did you make this, Mamo?"

The round head bobbed.

"For me?"

The head bobbed again.

"It's beautiful," she said with heartfelt sincerity. "Thank you."

The man's nervous gaze darted upward and held hers. His innocent brown eyes widened, and his mouth fell open. Mamo took a violent step backward, then nearly tripped on his own feet as he whirled away from her.

Goose bumps crawled over Jayna's arms as she watched him scramble and stumble along the corridor. Something had upset him when he'd looked into her eyes. Had he seen a difference in her the others hadn't yet?

"It's unbearable," Tiy sighed. "You should order that lunatic thrown into the street."

Jayna looked into Tiy's eyes, letting her get a good, long look in return.

The older woman's piqued expression wavered, and she had a moment's difficulty keeping her gaze level. "Well, you should. He's unstable at best."

Her stare had served only to raise the woman's defenses.

Tiy reclaimed her composure and turned haughtily. Shoving open the door Mamo had haunted, she awaited Jayna.

Jayna stepped in past her. The queen's chambers were identical to the king's in layout and basic furnishings. A cozy reception room led to the inner sanctum. The colors, however, were deeper, more comforting. Dark greens and blues covered the bed and chairs, maroon-and-blue rugs lay upon the floor. The statues and wall hangings reflected the cares of the ancient woman: the figure-gods of protection, beauty, and strength. An entire table near the side wall was devoted to the outer trappings of beauty. Jayna halted. Near the bowls and jars of makeup lay a bronze-handled mirror. She'd be able to see what she looked like. She could see what Mamo had seen and been so horrified by.

Would her own face reflect back at her, or would it be the green-eyed killer-queen's?

"Tiy—" Placing Mamo's statuette on a low cupboard, she turned around. With great effort, she spoke in slow, controlled tones. "I need some time to myself. This day has left me frazzled."

Tiy hesitated. "I sent your ladies to refresh themselves."

"I'll manage alone."

"Hareb's gathering the others near the pool as we speak. There's no better time, with Amony and his constituents holed up in his chamber."

Others? Jayna thought. How many others?

The older woman sighed. "Very well. Take a moment, but we'll be expecting you along shortly." Stepping forward, she grasped Jayna's shoulders. "Just remember. We almost did it. Next time you won't have to face Amony. Only his mourners."

Shock froze Jayna's face, hiding the horror that burst inside her at what the woman meant as encouragement. She forced herself to nod. She pulled away and walked stiffly to the far right door. Pushing through, she found herself in a lavatory, complete with a table and bowl for washing, and a pot set above sand for other needs. She stood staring at the crude toilet a moment, then ventured back to the main chamber. Tiy was gone.

The mirror lay on the table: her identity, for whatever a mirror could tell her of it. What others saw.

What Amony had seen.

She already knew this queen's body resembled her own, but what about her face?

Green eyes. Maybe her eyes were still brown. If she was a messenger, sent in her own Twenty-first Century form to warn Amony, everyone's eyes could be dimmed to the real Jayna. Everyone but the man-child's.

Or maybe this was the end for her. If she'd died in Amony's tomb, she could very well be just an afterlife bonus, of sorts. Amony's existence had looked a charmed one until his unnatural death. What more might he want than a queen who didn't long to spill his blood?

She walked slowly toward the table.

The bronze mirror felt cool and heavy in her palm. Curling her fingers tightly around the handle, she lifted it and looked in.

Chapter Three

Green. Bright, unmistakable green.

Am I dead?

Jayna pushed the mirror back to the tabletop.

What did it mean?

Was she a messenger sent to stop Amony's murder? And what—oh, terrible thought—what if she failed? Had she died in the tomb, only to face death again as a traitor? Was she doomed here? Surely the queen had been executed for her role.

I don't feel dead, she thought, and glanced around the luxurious room. *Only very far from home.*

She picked the mirror back up as if it were a viper, but once tamed within her grasp, she steeled her resolve and looked again.

Green. No matter how many times she'd look, her eyes would still be green.

The dark-lashes of the woman who stared back at her flickered in disgust. Her eyes—almond shaped, but not almond colored. She held the mirror back a little farther. Was the rest of her face the same? Different? Thin brows arched above her eyes. A thin, smallish nose her high school friends had always claimed to envy rested above too-full lips. A trade-off, she'd thought. No one had envied her lips, especially not herself.

Were they a little thinner, though? And her chin. The angle was different, nothing remarkable, a subtle rounding only.

Was there no significant difference between her and this queen?

The scar. She tilted her head and shoved her dark hair away from her temple. The hair felt strange, different. She pulled on it, and it came loose in her hand. A wig. The status symbol worn by all women of nobility. Her own thinner, softer hair coiled in a smooth bun at the back of her head.

Laying the wig aside, she looked in the mirror again. Her parents didn't know how she'd gotten the thin, inch-long scar on her temple. They'd said she'd had it from birth. She peered closer, turned her head this way and that, yet she couldn't find it. The scar was gone.

So that was it? The only substantial difference between her and this queen was a scar on her temple and a pair of green eyes?

Well, there's an inward difference, Jayna thought. Jayna Monroe wouldn't do what this queen had done. Jayna Monroe would go to the king, tell him what she knew, and stop his death.

Unfortunately, no matter what she felt inside, a green-eyed queen had plotted and killed her husband. And, for the moment, she was that woman. Unless she had some magic button to push that would zap her back to the tomb, she'd be a fool to go rushing to the unknown man and claim her involvement in such a conspiracy.

Would simply speaking the words of warning suffice to return her to her time? Would she ever be able to return?

She drew a shaky breath.

If speaking the warning didn't work, if she was doomed to remain here, or if the way back lay elsewhere, she could be asking for serious trouble. She had no idea if she could expect favor, or a burning at the stake. Would the Pharaoh pardon her, his wife, the one to come clean about the plot? Would he believe her if she told him what she knew?

Who would admit such a thing? He'd probably think she was insane.

What would Tiy think, or the man, Hareb?

That she needed a bricking?

She placed the mirror, face down, back on the table. Though her exchange with Amony had been brief, she'd gathered that he didn't entirely trust her. He'd questioned her initial reaction to his accident, suggesting that Hareb's version of her trauma was greater than what she'd displayed. And he'd wanted her out of his chamber when he was in such pain.

She'd have to wait. Unless she felt some—What, pull from the other side that might herald her return to life?—she'd have to wait and read the signs. Telling Amony about his future at this moment was tantamount to cutting her own throat.

She'd have to find out more about the relationship between the queen and her king. It wouldn't hurt, either, to find out more about these conspirators. She already knew about Hareb, Tiy, and Tiy's companion. How many more were there?

Tiy said there was to be a meeting at the pool. Would she be able to carry off her role? What if they asked questions only the true, green-eyed queen could answer? What if she drew suspicion on herself?

I'll defer to the trauma of the day, she thought. Thank you, Tiy. She put a hand to her forehead where a dull ache had begun to throb since Mamo bounded down the hall. Or I'll tell them I have a headache.

Lowering her arm, she took a deep breath and looked around the room. Pool. I've got to find the way back to the pool.

* * *

Tiy, Sefu, Desta, Roble and his wife Rana, Hareb, and Yera. Seven people involved, besides herself. High-ranking nobles in Amony's court. This was no light conspiracy, or personal vendetta. The Pharaoh's slaying was a plot of the grandest proportions.

Jayna sagged down on the bed and looked in the bronze hand mirror. "You're to blame for it, you witch." Green eyes sparked back at her. "Who are you, anyway?"

The queen remained silent.

Jayna tossed the mirror aside and gazed about the chamber—the queen's chamber, containing the woman's most personal possessions.

Jayna leaped up. Crossing the room, she threw open the lid of the chest that resided against the far wall. Clothes: dress after dress of linen and silk, some plain, some embroidered with fancy design. Green, blue, orange. All colors, all designs.

All moods?

She glanced at the table near the far wall. Closing the chest, she walked over to look at the collection of cosmetics: kohl, eye-shadow, rouge. Brushes, combs, perfumes. Bottles and bottles of perfume. The ancients were firm in their belief that body odor was equal to sin.

A strong sense of hypocrisy twisted through Jayna. "We wouldn't want to commit that little indiscretion, would we, Your Highness?"

With a snarl she swept the back of her hand across the tabletop. A knock sounded at the door before she could stop her arm from swinging. Pottery shattered on the floor. Bronze clanged and bounced. She stood very still, listening—shaking. What was this rage that consumed her? She'd never been a violent person.

When all was quiet, the knock sounded again.

Pushing her hair out of her face, Jayna took a deep breath and looked at the mess she'd made. No one had to know. She could clean it up before anyone saw it.

"Yes?" she called, then winced. Her headache had grown worse since the meeting at the pool. "What is it?"

"It's Atep, Your Highness. I'd like to speak with you about the Pharaoh."

Amony's physician.

Jayna rushed to the door, and stepped out, joining the man in the reception room.

"How is he?" she asked. "Will he be all right?"

"Not to worry." Atep put up a hand, his long fingers spread wide. "His injury isn't life threatening, but—"

He paused too long for Jayna's peace of mind. "But what?"

"He needs to stay off his feet for a few days and give his insides time to heal."

She nodded. "I see."

Atep shook his head. "He plans to attend the reception tonight. There's no keeping him abed. I've let him know I'll sanction it, if he moves as little as possible and retires early. I would..." He moistened his lips. "I beg of you to, please, see that he does this."

Jayna couldn't keep the trepidation from her voice. "What shall I do?"

Atep's face grew serious. "Accompany him to the dining room and walk him back out of it—early. He must put as little weight on his right leg as you can manage. His pride won't let him accept the arm of a help-man, but the people can't find fault in the Pharaoh enjoying his wife's companionship."

"No, they can't, can they?" Jayna followed the man's line of thought completely. The Pharaoh couldn't project his human frailty to the people. A Pharaoh, after all, was far above the common lot. And Jayna would help him. She would gather up her courage and face Amony again. After all, the key to getting out of here certainly lay with him. "I'll take care of the Pharaoh."

Atep nodded, his slim face bright with relief. "Thank you," he said, turning toward the door.

Did the court physician think he was asking more of the queen than she would like to give?

Jayna grasped the handle before he could touch it and looked into his eyes. "No," she said. "Thank you."

She pulled the door open. Atep stepped out and she shut it, then walked back to her inner chamber, her mind in turmoil.

What sort of wife was the queen that the man had to come, practically crawling, to ask that she do her husband the decency of offering her arm in his time of need? She turned and looked around the bedchamber, trying to find the essence of the woman whose body she shared. What kind of woman was the queen that she wouldn't look forward to accompanying Amony at a reception? Why, if Jayna were his wife, she would be thrilled. And honored. And excited.

But she wasn't Amony's wife.

"Why do you hide?" she demanded of the empty room.

Chapter Four

A quick examination of the far left door of her chamber yielded a spacious closet that held far more of the queen's wardrobe on hooks, shelves, and in a tall cabinet, than the simple chest had offered. Beyond, stood another door. She tried it and found it adjoined the sitting room and personal chambers of the queen's ladies.

The women were in attendance, getting ready themselves, for the feast to come. She bade them return with her. The queen's appearance wasn't going to go lacking tonight, not when she was expected to join Amony on his arm. *Does he know?* Jayna fretted. Quite possibly not, with the way Atep had presented the situation. She'd hurry and meet him before he left his chamber without her.

Two servants arrived, one to apply her makeup, one to clean from the floor those portions of her kohl, rouge, and eyeshadows that weren't salvageable. Her ladies helped her slip into a sheer, gold-trimmed gown, then fastened a short, airy cape over her shoulders. Displaying a myriad of necklaces and bracelets before her, they urged her to accept a triple strand necklace of orange-colored carnelian, matching earrings, and finely-twisted gold bracelets for both her upper and lower arms. She returned to the makeup woman's stool and allowed a shoulder-length wig to be placed on her head. Fitted with a gold band above the straight-cut bangs, the wig was tastefully braided into innumerable tiny strands.

No bad-hair-days for the queen, Jayna thought.

The woman then applied a pale cone to the top of the wig. Sweet smelling like the lotus, the cone would melt throughout the hot evening and impart its delicate scent to its wearer. Two of the ladies left to get their cones, and when they returned, Jayna watched, amused as they helped one another secure them atop their heads. What had always appeared so strange to her in books looked quite pleasant in reality—like the party hats at a New Year's Eve celebration, or a birthday, only these were gentler to the eye and exquisite to the nose.

The makeup woman held a mirror in front of Jayna's face. Kohl-lined green eyes stared back at her, eyes filled with excitement and fear. Her emotion, but not her color. She let her gaze move over the rest of her reflection.

I look beautiful, she thought. *The Queen and I.*

She nodded her approval.

The mirror lowered and she turned to her women. Their individual chats halted.

"You look wonderful, Your Highness. Like the sun in the sky."

While they showered her with praise, one woman left to answer a knock at the door. She returned seconds later, her young, pretty face pale. Jayna recognized her as the woman who'd run to the break this afternoon, sobbing at the news that Amony had suffered an accident. "The Pharaoh is here," she said, then added, as if not quite believing it, "At the door."

Jayna blinked. "He's here?"

"Yes."

"But I thought—" She'd thought she had to go to him. She'd thought she had more time to prepare herself, to face her nerves and get past them. He was a powerful man, and she had a dangerous tale to tell. How much time did she have, anyway, to divulge her secret?

An eternity? Was she just the new queen in some afterworld second chance for the Pharaoh? If that explanation for her presence here was accurate, she didn't appreciate not having a choice in the matter. She didn't appreciate it at all.

The mainstay of her life was a burning love for all things Egypt, so she couldn't hate being here in the thick and thriving of it. Were *she* to have a second chance, this day and age would be her wish. But she wouldn't will upon herself this dastardly role of killer-queen. She loathed the thought of violence.

Her heart picked up speed, and she glanced at the women as if they could rescue her from her dilemma. But it was too late. Amony was here. She had to go and hope the best possible opportunity to tell the Pharaoh what she knew would present itself.

Other than that, she thought, *it doesn't matter what I say. To him, I'm his wife of—how long*? At the pool, Sefu had spoken as if the reign was a new one. And the tomb in the valley was far from complete.

Straightening her spine, Jayna drew a deep breath. This was hardly a first date. To him, anyway. She would face him as the Queen, and under the Queen's power, she would walk him to the reception.

"Let's be on our way."

The sentry left his position to draw open the outer door. Jayna, with her ladies behind her, continued her slow, steady pace, floundering only once, and only inwardly, as she caught sight of Amony. He stood slightly in profile to the door, his slim, noble nose sliding elegantly past a high cheekbone, his dark hair hidden beneath the royal headdress that caressed a firm, determined jawline. He presented the picture of cool indifference, but as she neared the threshold, his head turned, his dark gaze moving from her sandaled feet up the length of her gown and over the swell of her bodice. No inch of her went unmeasured by his gaze. Her skin flushed with its passing. Warmth stole over her, a blush heightening the rouge on her cheeks. Her image of the calm, composed queen disintegrated beneath the perusal of this all-powerful, overly-potent male.

"Your Highness." She stopped before him and curtsied with trembling knees. The memory of her arms around his muscular torso assailed her as she straightened.

Unfathomable dark eyes gazed back at her. "The reception begins soon. Shall we go together?"

Had Atep informed him, then, that he should accept her helping hand? She opened her mouth, but couldn't speak. She tried to nod, but her head moved only the slightest degree. He understood her assent, nevertheless, for he held his arm out to her in courtly fashion. She glanced at the muscular forearm and found safer distraction in the twisted jade-and-gold band at his wrist. Nothing helped her to avoid the sensation of actually touching his arm, though, and her already racing heart leapt at the contact. This was no half-unconscious man, but one fully aware and charged with an electricity that vibrated through to her fingertips. In desperation, she willed her palm not to sweat. Not tonight.

They moved slowly down the corridor, the king's men and her ladies following a few paces behind. Though Amony carried himself remarkably erect for his injury, Jayna felt a hitch in his gait. His handsome lips were compressed, and she wondered if he remained silent out of pain, or out of a lack of closeness to his wife. Shouldn't he at least make small talk of some kind? What was the nature of the relationship between this king and queen?

Voices carried out through three open archways that revealed a portion of the dining room ahead of them. Four to five chairs each surrounded some twenty tables. Many guests were already present, awaiting their Pharaoh.

Studying the interior as they approached, Jayna endured a fresh batch of nerves. The meeting at the pool had gone well enough, but this large group of people overwhelmed her. Certainly she'd be expected to know many of the guests. Would she be able to pull off her charade?

That torturous thought came as her glazed vision swept the gathering, and in the same moment she should have looked down. Passing through the archway, a single stair-step required descending to join the dining room. She missed it.

A cry escaped her lips as she felt herself airborne. She pitched forward, but Amony's arm swooped round her, catching her. His stifled groan sounded in her ears as she slammed against his firm-body. Shaken, but on her feet at the edge of the not-so-great precipice, she twisted and looked into his eyes. Pain flickered there, and showed in the grim lines about his mouth.

"I'm sorry!" she moaned. "I'm so sorry. Are you all right?"

He nodded, the faint freckles on his nose seeming more pronounced against the pallor of his face. "I'm fine."

Jayna clenched her teeth. She was here to help the man, and she only brought him more pain. She shook her head—and realized that the dining room was now silent. Suspecting that all eyes were upon them, she closed her own eyes in embarrassment. This royal role was beyond her capabilities.

"Oh, what sort of queen am I?"

"The clumsy sort?"

Humor tinted Amony's words.

She forced her eyes open. His thick, bronze chest filled her vision. Tipping her head back to meet his gaze, she saw that a soft smile played about his handsome mouth.

Her mortification eased a small degree. "I'm sorry," she said again. "Truly sorry. I meant to help you—"

"Don't be sorry." The stirring smile retreated, but the corner of his mouth lifted, equally charming her as he added: "That blush of yours is worth a little twitch."

Settling her hand back into the crook of his arm, he guided her in a dignified descent of the simple stair. To her dismay, she realized his gait was slower and heavier than it had been in walking to the dining room.

"Yera—" The Pharaoh greeted a grinning man who sent all sentiments save contempt from Jayna's heart. She well-remembered the cold calculation of Amony's vizier, his right-hand man, from the meeting at the pool.

"Your Highnesses," Yera bowed. "Your guests have all arrived. I wanted especially for you to greet Hanif, so instrumental in the continued peace we enjoy in our southern province." With the words he urged forth an elderly gentleman who brought with him a woman of near-equal years. "Your Grace." Yera turned his traitor's gaze on her. "You, of course, know Farida."

Jayna stood frozen. Her thoughts so fully on the evil Yera, the very thing she'd feared upon entering the room happened. How well did she know the woman? She needed, at least, to reach out to her, but should she clasp her hand or embrace her lightly?

Amony stepped in front of her—and clasped Farida's hand. She'd let the moment draw out too long!

"The Queen has spoken of you often and with affection," he said. Stepping back, he twisted slightly and looked at Jayna, his brows lowered in a frown. His gaze searched her face as if she'd suddenly grown polka-dots on her cheeks.

Heat rose under her skin. Pursing her lips together, she turned her blush on the woman. "Farida, I'm so glad to see you." She took the woman's hands, and sensing the way the woman leaned toward her, realized she did know her well enough for an embrace. She performed the gesture.

While Amony conversed with the husband, Jayna exchanged pleasantries with the woman. Within moments another couple approached. And another. Finding safety in encouraging others to speak of themselves, Jayna adopted a cheerful mien and greeted all with enthusiasm. The queen's acquaintances wouldn't go slighted, and, she reasoned, those more distant could only appreciate a welcoming monarch.

With the entrance of servants bearing trays of fruit, Amony walked her slowly to a table where three other ladies sat. She knew current Egyptian fashion dictated that a man and wife didn't sit together at dinner, but she wished it weren't so. Any further understanding of this royal marriage was definitely on hold if she had to spend the evening on the ladies' side of the room while Amony joined the men.

"Your Highness," he said, relinquishing her arm.

She nodded carefully. "Thank you."

He moved away, his gait slow, and she agonized over her clumsy entrance into the room. He paused for a chat here and there, to rest himself, she was sure, then finally lowered into a chair at a table with several other men.

The first part of her night's duty was completed. Now she had to bluff her way through the remainder of the evening. As monarch she chose the option of a quiet evening listening to the women talk. For an Egyptologist, learning the minute details of their private lives proved a treat beyond compare. She almost forgot the strangeness of her presence here, so enthralled was she by the people and the actual manifestations of their customs. She ate from the dishes offered her, and sipped from her goblet only occasionally. The brew within the vessel was overly tart, making the veins in her forehead pound fiercely, and reminding her of the ache that hovered just beyond her thoughts.

She kept an eye on the king and noted that he drew more attention than just hers. The women of Amony's court weren't blind to his appeal. Handsome, powerful, the Pharaoh was irresistible to the eye. She couldn't understand how the queen could want him dead. He'd been so charming, teasing her when she'd made that spectacle of herself upon entering the room. From what she could tell so far, Amony was as kind as he was beautiful.

She should just tell him the truth and let the queen deal with the repercussions.

But I am the queen, she reminded herself with frustration. *And I don't deserve more torture, after those days in the tomb. I don't. I don't!*

Much later in the evening, she caught Atep's gaze upon her. The physician nodded toward Amony. She understood his meaning. For too long now, there had been a slump about the pharaoh's shoulders. He looked weary.

Jayna excused herself from her dinner companions and navigated the maze of tables and chairs. Her nervousness grew as the men at Amony's table turned to her. Now, Amony was sure to look—

His dark gaze found her, turning her knees to quivering liquid. She stopped before him and crouched low to speak for his ears only.

"We must go. Atep has given the sign."

She waited. Would he resist her?

He returned his attention to the men. "I must be leaving—" He pushed back his chair. Jayna rose as he got to his feet. Alarm rushed through her to see his face go pale with the movement.

"Tomorrow for the border check, then?" a man said, unaware of the frightful swaying in the king that completely absorbed her attention.

Afraid she was committing an error, but unable to see a better alternative, Jayna threw her arms around Amony's waist. "But you promised the day to me!" Clinging, her cry reaching his companions' ears, she helped him remain erect. A bit of color returned to his face and his gaze sharpened on hers. Had her ploy been ill-offered? She added, "Unless I'm mistaken."

"No, you're right," he said slowly. "I hadn't forgotten you." One hand braced on the table, the other around her shoulder, he turned to the man who'd spoken. "Let's save that for day after next. I've already made a promise to the Queen."

Jayna stepped back while he bade his farewells, but Amony kept her hand on his arm. Together, they walked out of the room at a brisk pace that surprised her. Once they were well out of sight, with only the guard and her ladies following, Amony slowed.

"Such thoughtfulness," he said, his voice ragged. "Gaining me a day of rest with my queen. How shall we fill it?"

Jayna noted the white cast arouhis voice low and nd his mouth that spoke of pain. "I should hope resting in your chamber," she said. "Will Atep be coming to see you tonight?"

He frowned. "I can count on it, I'm sure."

Jayna realized they were walking toward the corridor leading to her chamber, and she hesitated. As protective as Atep had been, she felt she should walk Amony to his room. "I should go the distance with you."

He paused beside her. "Should you? You'll come in then?" A bit of the pallor retreated from the handsome face. "Not many a gentleman allows a lady to escort him to his door. I'll have to walk you back."

Men and their ridiculous notions, she thought.

"Then, I'll come in," she said, relieved that he carefully re-routed them toward his chamber.

"I'm no danger with this limp."

His words surprised her.

"Your favor lies with weakness," he said. "I should have seen that in your love for Mamo." His gaze darkened. "You wouldn't come in if I weren't lame."

Confusion filled Jayna. Why wouldn't the queen enter his chamber while he was whole and well? Was he a danger to her? She'd wondered, in the tomb, if the king was abusive. Had he hurt the queen? Was this why she sought his death? As supremely perfect as the man appeared to be, such a horrific circumstance was the only reason Jayna could think of for the queen's treachery.

Amony opened his chamber door. Jayna stopped short of entering.

He turned and viewed her from the archway.

"Are you coming in?" He looked at his guard, who stalled and turned and inspected the ceiling. "You've got them confused. They don't know what to do."

A quiet talk between the royals seemed just the thing to bring Jayna closer to her goal, but she was suddenly wary. Did the queen have something to fear from him? Surely not tonight with his injury paining him and Atep due to arrive.

Was it only her imagination that his color had returned and he spoke with more energy? She let her gaze drop to his bare, sculpted, incredibly healthy-looking pectorals and wondered how long Atep would be.

"I think I'll leave you, after all," she said quickly. The Pharaoh's dark eyes flickered. Glancing away, she mumbled out an excuse. "You have your injury to think about."

"You've tricked me," he said, his voice low. "You escorted me to my door."

Tipping her head back, she braved his gaze. "I'm thinking of your health."

He stared down at her, his face stiff and unsmiling. "It's wonder enough that you graced my chamber this afternoon. Twice in one day is too much to consider."

Alarm tripped through her. Had she acted out of the ordinary? Should Tiy have prevented her from going to him, not pushed her into it?

His slim, dark brow arched slightly, then he leaned close, so close that the warmth of his body touched hers. His breath stole softly across her ear. "Or do you fear—the night?"

The mocking, whispered words scurried down her spine. He didn't step away, just let his softly issued taunt hang heavily between them. Her breathing quickened. She had to speak. She had to say something. So she answered from her heart, palpitating so near his heated, naked chest. "It may be the night."

He straightened slowly, relinquishing the vise his body held on her breathing space, but a sharp gleam entered his eyes. "Her Highness would answer another summons in the sun? Tomorrow's sun?"

Jayna's throat felt numb, immobile, and only force of will allowed her to murmur, "She might."

Her answer, vague though it was, frightened her. At the moment, any private meeting with this disturbing man struck her as out of the question.

Amony looked at her as if he didn't believe her answer. At last he said, "Come to my chamber for the morning meal."

His gaze searched her face while she sought a response. She could only nod.

He stepped back, and looked at the guardsmen. "Escort the Queen to her chamber."

"I—I have my ladies."

His dark gaze held hers. "And my guard."

She nodded and stepped away. Avoiding eye contact with any of the retinue, she made her escape down the corridor.

***

Tiy waited outside her chamber door, pacing back and forth in front of the guard. Jayna didn't speak as the woman followed her inside. The ladies crowded in behind Tiy.

"Go along and see to yourselves," Tiy told them. "I'll tend the Queen."

Jayna turned and met their questioning looks. The last thing she wanted was a little of Tiy's girl talk, but there seemed to be no way out. At her nod, the women curtsied and said their good-nights.

When the door shut behind them, Tiy clapped her hands together. "Bravo. Beautiful performance. The Pharaoh is surely fooled."

Jayna removed her wig with a trembling hand. "I'm sure he is."

"I'll need some of your jewels. Sefu and Roble are hatching a plan. I don't know what it is yet. Once they're certain of it, they'll tell us."

Not knowing what else to do, Jayna didn't stop the woman from rummaging through the queen's jewelry box. The headache that had threatened all day raged by the time Tiy left her.

Putting out the oil light, Jayna crawled into the large bed. Who, she wondered, would rise in the morning? Herself, or the queen? Had she lost her only chance to warn Amony?

Well-padded cushions met her tired body, and the silk sheet caressed her softly. She sighed and lay gazing at the strange darkness of the chamber, so different from her own bedroom in the sparse little apartment in Boston. Not that she spent much time there. Egypt was her love, and in Egypt she often, and easily, made her bed beneath a canopy in the open desert. She couldn't complain about this plush palace.

Her thoughts returned to Amony, and she winced. She couldn't do it. She couldn't think anymore for the agony that racked her brain. Lying very still, she let her mind go blank. The pain in her head eased, and gradually, she fell asleep.

Chapter Five

"Daren!"

Blood poured from a wound on the young man's neck. She stumbled toward him, screaming his name. He stretched an arm toward her and collapsed to the ground. A woman ran past her, then a man. Mother. Father.

Tears streamed down her face. Horror clawed at her chest.

"He's dead!" her mother sobbed over her brother's body. "He's dead!" Her voice rose to a piercing shriek. "*He* did this!"

"Who?" Jayna realized she'd moaned the question aloud when the elders' faces turned up to her. The venom that met her gaze sapped the breath from her lungs.

The people disappeared, leaving her standing alone.

"Me."

She looked up. Amony walked toward her, a slight smile on his lips. "You're looking for me."

He couldn't mean what she thought. She shook her head. "No."

"Yes." He continued toward her with that same, diabolical smile playing around his mouth. He stopped in front of her and wrapped his arms around her waist.

"No—" She pushed at him but his grip had already loosened. She stumbled beneath his sudden weight as he collapsed toward her, sliding down the front of her. A trail of bright red blood smeared her from neckline to waist. "No!" she screamed again.

The mighty Pharaoh crumpled to the ground. She reached down to him with blood-soaked arms.

"Amony!"

Wiping the blood from his face, she found herself staring into her father's aged countenance. The professor. And he was only sleeping. Relief soared through her. She removed his spectacles and his face softened, shifting into the gentler lines of the young man who'd first stumbled toward her, clutching his neck.

Daren was dead.

Still dead.

She screamed.

***

After the long, torturous night, Jayna awoke with her situation unchanged, but her heart and mind seriously altered. The fear Amony had hinted at in his wife was true. Last night, the queen's subconscious mind had screamed its way into her dreams. Though Jayna didn't know all the details, the queen believed Amony responsible for killing her brother. The horrible scene hadn't been just a dream. The queen had experienced it.

Jayna knew, without a doubt, that she need look no further for her answer as to why the woman wanted Amony dead.

Jayna wasn't a believer in 'an eye for an eye.' Amony didn't deserve to be killed, but neither was she up to facing a pleasant morning with the man her counterpart hated. The queen wouldn't meet with him in his chamber, neither would she.

Her ladies came to help her dress but she lay in bed, exhausted from her nightmare. "Go away, please. Come back later."

"Your chamberlain is due to arrive any moment, Your Highness."

"Who?" Jayna asked, her brain fuzzy.

"Hareb. Shall we send him away?"

"Definitely." She had no desire to see that man this morning, either.

The ladies turned to leave, but one dark-eyed woman with springy black hair hesitated. Her pretty face showed concern. "The dream again, Your Highness?"

So it was a recurring thing?

Of her ladies, this woman, Orisa, met her gaze most often, and returned her smiles more quickly. Hareb had said they couldn't be sure of the loyalty of her ladies. Loyalty to a killing wasn't what she wanted anyway. She needed some answers and the woman just might be able to provide them.

"Orisa, will you stay?" she asked. "I need to talk to you."

The priestesses left, and Orisa knelt at her bedside. "Your Highness?"

"I want to talk to you about—" Jayna moistened her lips. *What?* How could she go about this without exposing herself as an impostor? "My parents," she said finally. "I want to talk about my parents."

Orisa's gaze dropped. She studied the floor a moment. "What do you want to talk about?"

"What can you tell me?"

"So you know?" Guilt stamped itself upon the innocent face.

"Know what?"

Orisa pushed up and away. She busied herself straightening the cosmetics on the table. "They're back," she said. "Staying in Saqqara." Her dark gaze peeked quickly over to Jayna, then fled. "Your father's getting much better. His rages have ended, but he remains very contained."

Jayna thought of the anguished face from her dream and frowned. That last look from both the elders had held fury, as well as pain. Were the father's rages related to the son's death?

And why should her parents' presence in the nearby town of Saqqara surprise her? Why was her lady aware of it while she, evidently, wasn't? "How do you know so much, Orisa?"

Orisa's slim shoulders shuddered with a sigh. "Your mother has contacted me."

Jayna raised up on an arm. "Why would she contact you?"

Orisa turned to face her. "Am I not your cousin? Do I not care for you?"

The word 'cousin' shocked Jayna. She fought to recover. "Yes, of course. I didn't mean—" She broke off in frustration, and sat up. "Why didn't *Mother*—" the name came with difficulty "—contact me?"

"The fight, the feelings. But I have to tell you. She's forgiven you." Orisa pursed her lips together, then released a shaky sigh. "She's forgiven you because—" her lips tightened again, as if she couldn't say more, but she added in a rush "—she's come to believe that you married on false pretenses. To avenge Daren's death."

Jayna's blood seemed to turn to ice water in her veins. "In what way, Orisa?"

The woman hesitated, then said, "I don't know."

"What do you think?"

"I don't know. I mean, I don't believe it."

"But Mother does? What does she think I'm going to do?"

Anguish marred the pretty face. "I can't say it. It's too terrible."

The queen's own mother believed her capable of something too terrible to speak aloud? Murder, perhaps? Jayna lay back on the bed and groaned. "My head hurts."

"Shall I fetch Atep?" Orisa asked quickly, eager to be gone, it seemed.

"No."   Jayna pressed the back of her arm over her forehead, and waved a hand. "Don't. I'll be fine. I just need some sleep."

Orisa didn't move.

Pulling her arm back, Jayna looked at the doubtful face. "It's true. I promise. Come back later, and you'll see."

Orisa complied, leaving her in solitude. But Jayna wasn't alone. The faces of the three people—the queen's mother, father, and dying brother—haunted her.

The ladies returned a while later with a platter of fruit. Jayna moved around a bit to test her head. It no longer ached. A sudden commotion sounded outside the door, and one of the women went to see to it.

Amony's voice reached her through the reception room door. "This absence will not go unexcused."

The Pharaoh limped into her inner chamber at a furious, awkward pace. The sparkling-eyed Orisa and the elder of the ladies, Penda, stepped in his path. Jayna watched them with disbelief and affection. Didn't they fear the king? Their shoulders up, their chins high, they blocked his headlong charge toward her.

His Highness drew to a halt. The anger on his face softened, but didn't dissipate. "Excuse me, ladies."

The two wonderful women curtsied, but didn't budge.

His dark eyes narrowed. "I would speak with the Queen. You needn't fear for her, I promise you. I would only talk. Now, please. Step away."

The ladies moved hesitantly.

Amony nodded. "Thank you."

Jayna added a silent thanks and resolved to reward them in a more substantial way, for the Pharaoh couldn't maintain quite the same level of pique after such a polite exchange. He stepped in front of her, his color calmer, the firm line of his mouth a bit softer. "Your explanation, Your Highness?"

Jayna used the excuse she'd awakened to. "My head aches-"

"Your—" Amony's words twisted on his lips, then spilled forth in a growl. "Your stubbornness knows no bounds. You set this day. You will fulfill it."

"My head—"

"Can ache in my chamber," he said, his eyes glinting dangerously. "You will stand by your words. For once in your life, you will stand by your words." His voice lowered to a deceptive purr. "And you'll honor mine. Be in my chamber for the midday meal. Do you understand?" He barely gave her time to respond—so she thought—before he demanded: "Do you understand?"

"Yes," she said.

"Good." He picked up her neglected tray from the bedside table and pushed it into her hands. "Best sample what you can. It may be awhile before we find time to actually eat."

He left her to ponder what he meant. What would the royal couple do, alone in his chamber, to keep them too busy to eat? Would he press her? She was not his wife, not all his wife, anyway. Part of her was Jayna Monroe, Egyptologist virgin. Had the queen and king been intimate? Surely on their wedding night. But thereafter? With the way the queen felt about the king? Frightening thought—did he ever force her?

A vision of Amony's unclad chest and silky whisper sent a warm flush through her.

No. There would be no breakfast with the king today, and no lunch, either. Not until she could get her thoughts together.

She couldn't stay here, though. She'd have to go somewhere public where he couldn't limp in and threaten her.

Her ladies helped her dress, then stood back while the makeup woman, Maisha, did her face and hair. Jayna couldn't find fault in this situation of built-in friends offering her company whenever she desired it. However, the Pharaoh evidently didn't care what her ladies witnessed between them, thus they weren't safe companions. She dismissed them to do what they would for the afternoon, then left her chamber a minute or two later. She hurried past the sentry at Amony's door and emerged through the arches outside the pool.

As she'd hoped, a host of nobles lounged about the terrace. Though a few were of the very group she despised, *her group*, there were several unknowns. She went to join a couple who looked as if they wouldn't mind the intrusion of a third person. The woman and her husband watched the other nobles with an intensity that betrayed their wish to congregate in a more substantial way than merely sharing the same patio. Perhaps a chat with the queen would be just the thing for them.

"Your Highness," they greeted as she stepped near.

The man rose quickly to his feet, slightly ahead of his wife. "We attended the reception last night, but I'm sure you don't remember an insignificant merchant and his wife. I'm Edet and this is Kessie."

"Did you enjoy the reception?" Jayna asked as she sat down at their table. They stared at her, their mouths hanging open, before they realized they should answer.

"Oh, yes—" they answered together, in a rush, and sat back down, though on the edges of their chairs this time.

Jayna was acutely conscious of her role as queen until the couple relaxed and their discussion became friendly. She gazed around during pauses in the conversation and sought to remember the names of the few people she knew. The majority, she'd either seen or met last night. She studied them, trying to connect their faces with their names, and watched as, one by one, each ceased from his or her lounging, sipping, or talking. Three women rose in unison, quitting a small table. Gazes shot around the terrace and across the pool. A man tapped a woman on the shoulder, and with a tilt of his head, drew her gaze. She scrambled from her lounge and they strode off, patting a reclined man into wakefulness as they went.

Across the pool nearer Jayna, Roble's wife, Rana, lowered her goblet and headed for the archway to the palace. Jayna watched her go, confused by this strange migration.

Then she saw him.

The Pharaoh stood beneath the second arch, his arms crossed over his chest, his face dark with anger.

Chapter Six

The king's furious gaze had sent his subjects into flight. When that unrelenting, terrifying gaze fixed itself on her, Jayna understood completely, as they had understood. They had to go.

She, however, had to stay.

Her heart struck up a wild tempo against her ribcage. She'd underestimated the king. He didn't need to debate the disadvantages of storming in among his people and threatening her. All he had to do was look at them and make the terrace as private as his chamber.

What would he do?

As he strode forward, slowly, his pace betraying the slightest limp, anger radiated from him. She wanted to run, but she couldn't move. His raw power paralyzed her with fright. She'd made the wrong decision. She should have put him off somehow. Standing him up had been a huge mistake.

He stopped an inch in front of her, forcing her to tilt her head to look up at him. The seconds ticked by as he stared down at her. Finally, his mouth twisted. "You looked the concerned and loving wife for a most important day in your Pharaoh's life. The people all know, by now, of our special day together, of your wifely devotion before we return to our mutual duties. Well done, my Queen."

Jayna searched for her voice, and found a strained imitation of it. "I don't know what you're talking about."

"The chill about you ebbed when you thought I'd died, didn't it? How to recover, though, at the bad news that I lived? I count it somewhat to your character that it actually occurred to you to play concern."

Amony raised his hand and servants brought out trays of food. "I'll have what you promised." He gestured for her to sit, then settled in the chair across from her. "I could have had my servants bring you to my chamber, but I feared you might be bruised in your resistance." His brow raised. "You would have resisted?"

Jayna didn't answer.

His gaze lowered to the table. "You see, I care for your flesh. I wouldn't see you hurt."

Tentatively, she said, "I don't want you hurt, either."

"Is that so?" He stared at her, then nodded. "It would be difficult to have to endure another day such as yesterday. The effort of showing concern, actually stepping foot in my chamber. How long has it been since you've been there?"

Jayna looked away. How should she respond? Finally, she murmured the truth, "I don't remember."

"Neither do I," he said. "I find it interesting that you chose yesterday to honor a summons of mine, even to the extent of coming to my chamber."

"Is that why you summoned me?" Jayna asked, feeling her defenses rise. "To see if I would do it?" Amony didn't respond. "For what reason?" she asked.

The Pharaoh lifted his fingers from the table top in a casual gesture. "This hysteria Hareb spoke of intrigued me."

"I was much calmed by then," she said. "Naturally."

"Naturally," Amony repeated, giving a wry twist to the word. "Perhaps the man exaggerated a bit. Perhaps 'hysterical' was too strong a word for how you were feeling."

Jayna's heart thumped chaotically in her chest. Did he know about his wife's evil plan for him?

"I was upset," she said.

"Upset?"

"Shocked!" she elaborated. "Frightened." Fear rushed through her at this very moment. "Do you doubt me? Wouldn't your wife feel these emotions?"

"I suppose if she felt them," he said, his gaze intent, "I would see them last, to some degree, beyond the first moon. You must have experienced some deep trauma to have so obediently gone to my chamber and meekly played the dutiful wife for the rest of the evening."

Determined to set aside suspicion, she leaned toward him with a query. "But it wasn't upset, or fear for you that I felt?"

"Fear *of me* might put it in better perspective."

She stiffened. "Why would I fear you?"

"On a typical day, you don't. Evidently."

A sudden dryness assailed Jayna's mouth. Was he onto her? Did he suspect she had something to do with his accident and had presented herself to learn if a reprisal was forthcoming?

"Yet I feared you yesterday?" She willed her voice not to shake. "This is why I came to you, and stayed with you throughout the evening?" With a confidence she scarcely felt, she chided, "Your reasoning makes no sense."

Relief rushed through her when Amony's gaze fell away and he sat back in his chair to munch on a ripe, purple grape. His doubts she blamed on Tiy for making her go to Amony's chamber when it was a noteworthy thing to do. At the very least, she should have counseled her to arrive late. Jayna could only think the woman's guilty conscience had prompted her in the decision to make the queen go to his chamber.

Acutely fearful of drawing Amony's attention back to her, she reached out and selected items from the tray. He said nothing, so she began to eat.

Her belief that they had the terrace to themselves soon proved wrong. She caught sight of a figure beyond the palms and watched, waiting to identify the person who would defy Amony's obvious wish to have his subjects gone. A tingle of alarm ran through her. Was this to be another set-up? Was Amony's back safe?

As soon as her fear rose, it fled. The intruder was Mamo. A new concern welled within her. If Amony saw the man, how would he react? Would he glare at the sensitive one, or would he shout? The man's fragile psyche didn't seem strong enough to withstand a broadside of Amony's power.

She pretended not to notice him, but soon realized that the boy-man inched nearer. Didn't he understand the trouble he could get himself into?

Amony glanced over his shoulder.

She'd been too obvious.

Ducking her head, she chewed a piece of cucumber. A moment later, she peeked carefully up. Amony continued to eat, his gaze on the horizon beyond her. She watched Mamo circle around the end of the pool and navigate the chairs and tables. What did he want? Why was he coming so close to the king on this day when the entire court had been banished from the area? Had he no concept of the king's wrath?

Amony glanced over his shoulder again. He'd caught the direction of her interest once more. He had to have seen Mamo this time, but he didn't look angry. To her surprise, he twisted around on his chair.

"Mamo. Come here."

Would he give the poor man a stern word, now?

Mamo approached with remarkable ease. Shy as he was with her, a woman he had seemed to trust, he was far more confident in approaching the king. He shook not at all, and the downward cast to his face didn't include his eyes. He looked the king square in the face, then stopped beside him.

"What is that you have?" Amony asked, his voice as natural as if he were speaking to one of his noblemen.

Mamo glanced her way. Jayna smiled and was pleased that he smiled back at her. However, he cradled his arm in such a way that, as he showed Amony what he held, she couldn't see. Amony viewed the object, then his gaze raised to her. He appeared to be studying her face, then his gaze lowered again. Mamo, too, looked her over, then returned his attention to what he hid from her view.

Amony nodded. "You're a master artisan, Mamo. I should set you to work in my temple."

Mamo withdrew his private artwork.

"Would you like that?" Amony asked. "You could join the others, or work on your own, if you'd only keep the foreman apprised of your collection."

Pleasure lit the man's childish face, but he bit his lip as if troubled.

Eyes narrowed, Amony studied him. "You only have to ask the man for the supplies you need. I'll let him know that you may approach him. Just tell him what you want, or point it out, whatever you prefer. Of course, you'll need to be near the temple for the bigger works. We'll go down together. You can look the place over. If you see a workspace that suits you, it'll be yours."

Mamo nodded, eager, then he glanced at Jayna, and his expression fell a bit. "But—what 'bout room here?"

"I wouldn't separate you from those you care for. Your room will always be available anytime you choose to have it."

As Mamo walked happily away, Jayna stared at the handsome king. This was the man who'd killed another in cold-blood? Could a man be so thoughtful and yet so evil? It didn't seem possible.

Of course, who knew better than she how gorgeous Amony's tomb had turned out to be? Was it possible Mamo had carved those beautiful images of Amony? His statue of Hathor was perfect. He of anyone would be the artist to so capture the handsome Pharaoh. Amony would want to coddle the man capable of sending him into the afterlife with such beauty. Was that all this kind gesture was? The ploy of a rich man to get what he wanted?

Amony sipped from a slim goblet, relaxed and quiet while Mamo cheerfully settled himself in the shade of a nearby palm tree.

Jayna felt awful.

No matter what had happened in the queen's life, this conspiracy to murder Amony was wrong. The queen had to work out her loss and resentment in some way that didn't end in death.

The thought titillated her.

Is that why I'm here? To bridge the gap between them? Show Amony the way to his wife's forgiveness? But what way is that? How could the queen have married him if she believed him responsible for a loved one's death?

The revenge factor. The woman had meant to get back at Amony from the beginning. The heart of the matter lay in just how to get beyond that long-standing vengeance.

She studied the king so intently that it came to her as a surprise to realize he watched her in return. Their gazes met and she blushed. Picking up her goblet, she took a sip, then lowered it before glancing back at him. He still watched her.

She shifted in her chair and self-consciously moistened her lips. Finally, she averted her face. "Your Highness."

"Yes?"

She'd spoken from her discomfort, hoping he would leave off his regard. She'd failed, for his dark gaze still rested on her. "Do you have something on your mind?" she asked.

"Yes."

He added no more to the simple response, just reclined and stared, his arm resting in calm confidence on the table.

"You're making me uncomfortable," she said.

"You needn't be," he said. He left off his regard of her while he took a drink from his goblet, but his gaze returned promptly and with an intensity that sent a warning tingle through her nerves. "We're in far too public a place. Unless you've arranged something."

He shifted to glance around the deserted terrace, and Jayna's heart jerked in alarm.

"Mamo—" She thrust an arm toward the man huddled beneath the palm tree. "Mamo's here."

Her hurried claim had barely left her mouth when Amony laughed.

She stiffened, surprised. Was he only toying with her? Had she misjudged the desire in his eyes?

"I jest, my Queen." His short laugh dissolved and a distant sort of humor played across his handsome features. His mouth twisted at the corner. "I content myself with looking."

He did? Or he would for the moment? Jayna struggled beneath the complexity of this marriage. How did the queen endure this relationship? How did she feel about Amony's teasing?

Realizing how tense she held herself, she tried to relax back in her chair.

"I can still see you from there," Amony chided.

"I wasn't trying to—"

Dark eyes sparkled over a flashing grin.

Jayna's breath left her in a whoosh. The effects of the dream had worn off, and she was finding the belief that this man was a murderer difficult to sustain. He'd been so touchingly kind with Mamo. He would have been within a Pharaoh's power to punish her ladies for blocking the way to her, yet he hadn't even spoken a harsh word to them.

Truthfully, even she had incurred his wrath and come out unscathed.

Still flushed from the man's flirtation, she admired his handsome face.

Was it possible the dream was wrong? Had the king not killed the queen's brother? She had to find out the details behind the story.

If it turned out he was behind the killing, she'd do him in herself.

The thought alarmed her, bringing with it the memory of the intense rage she'd felt when she'd swept the top of her makeup table clean. She couldn't allow herself to think that way, not even as a joke. Folding her hands primly in her lap, she met Amony's gaze and smiled nicely.

A frown built on his brow as he watched her.

Another's voice sounded. "Your Highness?" Atep drew their attention as he passed through the archway. "Oh, good afternoon, Your Grace." He bowed before Jayna, then turned to the Pharaoh. Though his manner was cheerfully respectful, a thick tension edged his voice. "I hate to interrupt your afternoon, but there is an important matter that must be seen to in your chamber. If I could tend the matter without you, I certainly would, and to the best of my abilities, I assure you." He leaned forward, almost pleading. "But I can't do this without you. I need you to return to your chamber."

Jayna blanched. The healer wanted Amony back in bed. He probably hadn't wanted him out of it in the first place.

"Your Grace..." Atep turned to her, and Jayna roiled in guilt.

"I'm coming," Amony said quickly, making Jayna wonder if his swift acquiescence had saved her from a chastising. He rose, albeit slowly.

Jayna got to her feet.

Atep glanced between the two of them.

Embarrassment held Jayna's tongue.

Amony's gaze moved over her face one last time. "Enjoy your afternoon."

She nodded.

Chapter Seven

The terrace remained empty and silent except for the small sounds of a chisel moving over stone. Jayna turned and looked at Mamo. He glanced up at her, then returned to his work. Stepping around her chair, she walked carefully near him. When she was only a few feet away, he curled up his knees to obstruct her view of his project. She halted there.

"May I speak with you, Mamo?"

He nodded.

"You're not afraid of the Pharaoh, are you?"

Thick brows drew together in displeasure.

"I'm not suggesting you should be," Jayna said quickly. "I'm just surprised, I guess. I mean, goodness, sometimes I'm afraid of him."

Mamo shook his head. "Queen no fear. Mamo no fear. Never."

"Never?" Jayna asked before she could help herself.

"Always good. Always."

"Hmm." Jayna frowned. "How long have you known the Pharaoh, Mamo?"

"Since he crowned."

"Oh," Jayna murmured. Not very long.

"Before that, I knew the gen'ral."

She frowned. "The general?"

"Boy, then gen'ral, then Phay-ro."

"Oh," she said again, surprised. Understanding was slow in coming, but it was coming. "You've known the man a very long time."

"Good boy."

She watched, thoughtful, as Mamo continued chiseling. So Amony had been a good boy? What about Amony as a general? His tomb had depicted a great many war scenes.

She thought of the queen's brother.

Daren. She rolled the name over in her mind.

Daren had died before her and Amony's marriage, thus before Amony's kingship. While he was still a general, then. Had Daren's death been war-related? Had there been a battle involving Amony as the general?

No. If the dream was to be believed explicitly, Daren had died in the family courtyard from a freshly-delivered wound. If Amony was to blame for the killing, the two scenarios didn't add up. A general important enough to become Pharaoh wouldn't sneak around and lay in ambush for a single man.

Would he hire another to do the job?

She cringed at the possibility. Another talk with Orisa was in order. Maybe her cousin knew more of the details.

Watching Mamo chisel for another moment, she felt a sense of disquiet settle in her chest. He'd been so quick to defend Amony. What about her, the woman known as a killer for the past four thousand years?

"Mamo?" The man's gaze darted up at her. She started to change her mind about asking, but she had to know. "Are you afraid of me? You seemed frightened by me in the hall yesterday. Did I frighten you in some way?"

Mamo dug his head deeper and chiseled faster.

"You won't talk to me about it?"

She waited, but he didn't answer.

Finally, she sighed. "I'll leave you be."

***

"What qualities did we most share, do you think, in our youth?"

Orisa laughed and continued brushing Jayna's long hair. "Trying to figure out why you're Queen and I'm a mere priestess? It isn't difficult, Jayna." For the first time since Jayna could remember, the woman used her given name. "You're beautiful, always have been. You're bright, always have been." Her cousin walked around the chair and squinted down at her. "And you used to be a lot of fun."

"Used to be?"

Orisa gave a lopsided, sad sort of smile. "I'm sorry. You've just been so serious and silent since Daren died. I thought when you came to live with us that we'd be closer than sisters." Jayna knew she'd reacted outwardly, as well as inwardly, for Orisa thrust up her hands. "Don't misunderstand me. I love being a part of your ladies. It's just that..." Orisa bit her lip, as if she were saying too much.

Jayna reached out and grasped her hand. "Go on, please. I want to hear what you have to say." She released her cousin's fingers slowly.

Melancholy dimmed Orisa's eyes. "It's just that we're even less cousins, somehow, than we ever were. It saddens me. We had so much fun. You were so happy. I thought your marriage would bring you back to us. You were so—different—once you met Amony. It wasn't your true self, but I thought it was a start."

A start? Jayna thought. Orisa's words confused her. Meeting Amony had brought more of her happiness to the fore? How could that be?

"How was I different?" she asked.

"You were—" Orisa laughed "—nervous, to be sure. But almost happy, despite the tension."

Happy? Had she been happy merely because her plan to kill Amony was underway?

"And now?" she asked.

"You're serious again," Orisa said. "And so taut, I'd sometimes swear a simple touch would snap you in two."

Is that what happened?

Jayna's brain seemed to slam against her skull as the internal voice that was not her own echoed through her thoughts. Pressing her fingertips to her forehead, she closed her eyes. The blood inside her skull pulsed furiously, leaving her dizzy and confused.

"Are you all right? You don't look well."

Warm hands grasped hers.

Opening her eyes, Jayna looked to her cousin, who'd dropped to her knees beside her. With sturdy concentration, she thrust aside thoughts of that other voice. She would get through this. Questions needed answering.

She swallowed heavily. "Why did Daren die?"

"We can't know that. We'll probably never know."

"What do my parents believe?"

Orisa bowed her head and wouldn't meet her gaze. "You know that as well as I."

"I want to hear it from you."

Sad eyes raised to look at her. "They haven't changed in that regard. They still believe Amony found Daren a threat."

A threat? Her parents believed Daren had died because he was a threat to Amony? In what way? She couldn't come right out and ask without revealing her ignorance.

She tried another tack. "And you? What do you believe?"

Orisa shook her head. "I don't know. The campaign was over. Amony was to be Pharaoh. I don't believe your brother would have challenged him, but—" her slim shoulders rose and fell in a shrug "—I don't know enough of men and wars to say."

Her brother—the queen's brother—challenged the Pharaoh? Why? For what?

Jayna shook her head. "What would Daren have gained by challenging Amony?"

Orisa shrugged again. "He'd surely be vizier."

Vizier? Second in command only to the Pharaoh? It didn't make sense that Amony would find him a threat, then. Yera was vizier. Had Daren been a threat to Yera?

Daren had died through foul play. She didn't dispute that. But the gut feeling that Amony was innocent of this atrocious act settled deeper. He couldn't have done it. He wouldn't have ordered it. Her brother's murder had been the attack of a coward, and Amony was no coward.

But Yera? That man was a traitor. This much she knew.

She needed to know more, but she sensed she'd drawn all she could from her cousin without turning questions and suspicion on herself. "I'd like to speak with my parents."

"Your father might not be able to withstand seeing you," Orisa cautioned.

"I want to see Mother."

"She'd like to see you."

"Why didn't she have you tell me they were here?"

"Because of the fight you had over your marriage." Orisa took a deep breath. "She's had a change of heart, and came to watch over you. To make sure you don't do anything you can't get yourself out of."

Like kill the Pharaoh?

"Will Mother come here?"

"You'd risk having her here?"

"What do you think she would do?"

True worry filled her cousin's eyes. "She couldn't keep quiet, Jayna."

Jayna thought of the hatred she'd seen in the dream-woman's eyes just before Amony showed up. Her mother believed the queen's husband guilty of killing her son, driving away her husband's sanity, and, most likely, seducing her daughter.

"Can you arrange a meeting for us at some midpoint?"

"Yes."

"How long will it take?"

"If you don't have need of me, I can go immediately."
"You have to go, yourself? We can't send a messenger?"
"She doesn't trust anyone but me."

Chapter Eight

A profound sense of sadness lingered with Jayna well into the evening. Knowledge of her role as a woman who would kill for any reason, save self-defense, ate at her. Slumping against the wall of the wardrobe, she slipped off her bracelets. Where did one go to escape oneself? Or one's alter-ego? All afternoon, she'd anticipated a return of the voice within her mind. Confusion kept her thoughts solidly blocked.

Sluggishly, she raised her arm and placed her jewelry on top of the tall cabinet. The door to the ladies' chambers opened at the same moment. Penda peered in.

"Did you put your jewelry up there, again?" the woman clucked.

"I alwa—" Jayna stopped herself. This wasn't her bedroom in Boston where she always shoved her jewelry on top of the tall, standing clothes closet.

The woman raised on her tiptoes and felt around the top of the cabinet. "You truly have." She drew back a fistful of jewels. "I wondered where this was."

Jayna stared at the amethyst necklace. She'd never seen it before.

"And this." The woman plucked out a red bracelet and chuckled. "I should have thought to check up here. I haven't done a collection in a while, I guess. Well, let me put these away, and I'll help you change for bed."

"No," Jayna said quickly. She was definitely not ready for the solitary confinement of bed and the risk of horrifying dreams. "I was thinking—yes." She nodded. "I was thinking of taking a walk."

"A walk? Where?"

Jayna shrugged. "On the terrace, I suppose."

"Let me put these away, and I'll join you."

"Actually," Jayna put out a hand. "I'd like some time by myself. I'll return shortly."

Alone, but beneath the watchful eyes of the sentries stationed about the corridors, she made her way to the terrace.

Night had fallen, leaving the terrace empty for the second time that day. A sky of black velvet and diamond-bright stars draped high above. Wandering between the palm trees, Jayna willed some of the night's peace to come to her.

Nassor came, instead. The man who'd walked her out of Amony's chamber after his injury. Court gossip had brought her up to speed on this charming ladies' man and put her on protective guard. He stepped out of the arches and performed a slight bow. "Your Highness."

"What are you doing out here so late?" she asked.

"I couldn't sleep," he said. "You neither, I see?"

"No."

He placed an arm around her back the way he had on escorting her from Amony's sickbed. At first she felt surprise, then realized if he was comfortable enough with the gesture beneath the king's eyes and in front of his retinue, there was probably no harm in it now.

"You have much on your mind?" he asked.

Looking at him, she sighed. "I'm a bit confused, I guess."

"Why is that?"

"I don't think I can explain it."

"You can tell me anything, you know. I may play the role, but I'm very serious inside."

Jayna knew what he was talking about. The handsome Nassor did truly live up to the charming, flirtatious ways the women spoke of.

She stared out at the bright lotus blooms that floated on the surface of the pool. "Do you ever wish you could drop the pretense and be yourself?"

"Yes, I do," he said softly, drawing her gaze. "Our hearts have many needs we can't fulfill, don't they?" He brushed a tendril of her hair back from her face and his hand stayed to caress her cheek. "Needs we can't even speak aloud. Sometimes I tire from the effort. Do you tire, Jayna?"

Suddenly uncomfortable, Jayna took a quick step backward.

What was he saying? And why had he touched her so gently? Was there something more between her and this noble than there should be?

She rejected the thought quickly. He was handsome, there was no doubt of that, but nowhere near as handsome as Amony. Was he handsome enough, though, for a woman who hated her husband? He was, actually. Nassor, with his good-looks and wealth could have any woman he wanted.

Except the Queen of Egypt.

The queen might enjoy his company from time to time, but she wouldn't enjoy his attentions. At least not while Jayna ruled the roost. She waited for an answer within herself, some twinge of denial, some conflicting sense that the man's attentions were acceptable to the queen, but it didn't come. She wouldn't heed such a sign, anyway.

"Don't turn from me," he said. "We're alike, you and I. We need each other. No one understands the way we do." His hand slid warmly over her shoulder, tickling the fine hairs at her nape.

The gesture was right, the man, wrong. "I—"

He lifted her hand and pressed a kiss to her palm. "You're my Queen, and yet I have a friend in you no other can fill. I'm your servant first, but always your friend. Whatever you need from me, whatever you ask of me, it shall be done. Anything."

Was it so unusual that the court playboy should offer himself to the queen? For a man who treated all women to the full extent of his charm, he would be amiss to neglect the queen. Having put the matter into perspective, Jayna smiled. With reserve.

"The Queen thanks her noble," she said. "Now I would like to go back inside. Do stay and enjoy the air."

She left him quickly and didn't turn back.

In the safety of her lone chamber, she looked at the bed with reluctance. Penda returned to help her change, and Jayna kept her talking until the older woman yawned. She could no longer put off the inevitable.

Alas, the night proved she'd had nothing to fear. Her dreams were innocent: sitting on a flat, mud-baked roof, catching the early evening breeze, the pleasure of her brother's arm around her as he snuggled her against him. She smiled in her sleep, reveling in the warmth around her, the love. Until a distant noise roused her, drawing her, still half asleep, from the bed.

Scarcely aware she was doing it, she drew a thin robe over her shoulders and stepped out of her room. Wandering the corridors, she neared Amony's apartments—and saw a skirt flick through Amony's door.

Shani! The form belonged to Shani, her lady, the priestess who'd cried so at the news Amony had been hurt.

Jealousy raked through Jayna's breast. Violent jealousy turning to anger. No more would she tolerate this. Shani's doe-eyed looks at Amony, her absences when she called her ladies.

The emotions coursing through her made Jayna gasp for breath. The queen had followed Shani here before, and it hurt her terribly.

Jayna woke fully beneath the pain.

This carousing on the part of the king was a hindrance to the royal relationship, and she wouldn't allow it. She'd stop it.

She saw the guard's arm move as she approached, his fingers folding under...

"Don't do it," she ordered, stopping his knuckles a hair's breadth from the wood. The man's arm returned to his side.

"You let her in," Jayna said. "On whose order? Or is it a standing order that pretty women come and go as they please in the Pharaoh's chamber?"

The guard said nothing. She didn't expect him to. She had already said too much, herself. The man was a servant to the Pharaoh, not a snitch.

She stepped around him and pushed the door open. "Don't move," she ordered the interior guard, then pushed through that door, too.

A single oil lamp highlighted the two figures in the center of the room who stood with their arms entwined. Envy shot through Jayna's heart to see the woman in Amony's embrace.

Shani snatched free of the man who let her go easily. Guilt and horror marred the priestess' beautiful face.

"You're dismissed," Jayna said. "Get your belongings and get out of this palace."

"I'm sorry, Your Highness. Please—"

Jayna held no room in her heart for the woman's pleadings. "Go," she said coldly.

Shani fled the room.

Jayna looked to Amony. His startled gaze mellowed to an intent watchfulness. She turned, disgusted, intent on leaving at once.

Amony started for her. "Don't run away from me!"

A strange noise and a grunt of pain met Jayna's ears. She glanced over her shoulder, then whirled around completely. Amony lay face down on the floor. Evidently, he'd put too much weight on his bruised hip, and his leg had given out.

She rushed back to him. "Are you all right?" She kneeled down to him. "Amony?" He didn't move, didn't make another sound. "Amony?" Worried, she placed her hands gingerly on his thick side, and leaned over to peer into his face.

A single dark eye looked back at her.

"The wife of the Pharaoh of Egypt favors a weak man," he moaned. "It's my curse."

Relief soared through her that he was well enough to speak. Her anger reclaimed its righteous place in the fore of her mind. "Let me help," she said stiffly.

Laying her arm along his shoulders, she placed a hand on his chest and tried to push and pull at the same time to aid his momentum. With a groan, he rolled and lay on his back, his eyes closed.

"Shall I send for the healer?"

His eyes opened. "I'll be fine. I just need a rest, first."

She nodded.

He looked at the ceiling, then sighed. His gaze returned to her for a quiet moment. "Nothing passed between us."

Resentment rushed through her. "I interrupted this time. There have been others."

Amony shook his head. "She's been wishful, but I haven't touched her in tenderness."

"You're a rough lover?"

"Nor in roughness." His dark gaze delved into her eyes. "We've never been intimate. I swear it to you. I was telling her to leave when you came in."

Jayna stared into the dark depths of those eyes. Could she believe him?

"Does the thought that I'd be with another truly upset you?" he asked. "You're the Great Royal Wife. Lesser wives should pose no threat to you."

She pulled back from him in outrage. "Do you think to win your wife's heart with such talk?"

His eyes narrowed on her as jealousy gnawed at her chest.

Why? Why should the idea of Amony taking other wives hurt so?

The answer came in doubles. The queen wouldn't want her husband to find pleasure outside his marriage to her, a marriage made only to torment him.

And, as far as Jayna was concerned, a king interested in other women would find the wife who'd predict his death far more expendable.

"Let's get you on your feet," she said firmly.

She backed away, but his arm swept around her and pulled her close. She halted with a gasp, her breasts crushed to his chest, her face only inches from his.

"Don't go," he said softly. "Stay with me." Heat filled his eyes, then his gaze dipped with longing to her mouth. "I want you with me. You. No one but you."

Desire like Jayna had never felt before washed through her. His flesh was so warm, his lips so near. All she had to do was lean just a little closer and their mouths would meet.

Her body would belong to the king before the night was through. Would the Queen appreciate that, the giving of her body when her heart cried out for his death?

Jayna twisted free of the warm arm enveloping her. This man wasn't hers for the taking.

Thrusting herself to her feet, she hurried toward the door to call a helper to assist the Pharaoh to his bed.

Chapter Nine

"We're going on a trip," Roble said, his eyes alight. "A half-day's journey along the Nile in which anything may happen, followed by two days at Bene's estate. It's a virtual jungle up there, I tell you. We should come back empty handed, if you know what I mean."

Jayna lowered her gaze to her lap.

"Bene isn't an ally, though," Desta objected.

"It doesn't matter," Tiy said. "Nothing will be done in his presence."

"Jayna." Roble called her name, forcing her to look him in the eye. "Your role will be to stay near Amony and keep the others out of the way and out of sight. We're working on a plan or two, but we'll seize any opportunity available." He looked around the circle of conspirators. Only Yera was absent, his innumerable duties as vizier preventing him from attending the meeting, as well as participating in the planned trip. "Who's to say a moment alone on the bow, no one looking, couldn't bring a death blow? The Pharaoh could go over the side and not be missed for some time."

Hareb could barely contain his excitement. "He won't come back alive."

As soon as the meeting concluded, Jayna marched to the Pharaoh's council room, her stomach churning with revulsion for each and every member of the group who'd congregated in the garden. She had to tell Amony the truth, and quickly.

She stopped before the guard. "I need an audience with the Pharaoh. Immediately."

The man stepped inside, leaving her to wait in the hall. Jayna clasped her hands together to still the shaking that suddenly besieged them. Would speaking the words of warning suffice to save Amony, then set her free to return to her life? How long did she have before being found in the tomb? Eternity? Was she already dead? She had so much to do yet, analyzing the evidence of this Pharaoh in the sweltering Egyptian sand.

She shook her head at her thoughts.

She'd devoted the last year of her life to finding the tomb of the man who now called her wife. What importance lay in analyzing the artifacts in his tomb when she actually lived her life alongside him? Ate lunch at a table across from him? Trembled in his arms at the thought of his kiss?

Doubt washed through her.

She wrung her hands.

Was telling Amony the truth such a good idea? What was her rush to get back to her life, or back to the tomb where black death might await her? What was her hurry to face the man who, in all fairness, could see her burned at the stake for her treachery?

To save his life.

Jayna looked nervously down the corridor to her right, then her left.

She only wanted to save him.

And herself.

She groaned at her foolishness in coming here. The distance between the royal couple was too great to withstand such a confession as she had to make. The king wanted his wife in a physical way, but since when did physical attraction equal trust, or affection? Her original gut feeling provided the best, and only, course of action. Unless she felt Amony in immediate peril of losing his life, unless she felt the Great Hand who had brought her here calling her back, she had to remain silent on the queen's guilt. The queen's life, and her own, depended on it.

She turned to flee.

The door swung open, emitting the guard and the Pharaoh. The bulky servant moved aside, leaving the leaner-bodied king standing in front of her. Majestically outfitted for his morning court affairs, Amony wore his official headdress, twin bands of curving gold on his upper arms, and a pleated linen kilt around his hips. The air of authority with which he conducted his affairs emanated powerfully from him.

His dark eyes narrowed on her. "You wished to speak with me, Your Highness?"

"Yes," she said. Now she had to think up something, fast. "Uhh—" What could she say?

The door behind them opened and a harried-looking fellow emerged. "Your Highness, I hope I didn't offend you. I meant no harm."

Relief soared through Jayna as the door opened again, and two more men joined the first. All looked to their king with worried faces.

"You must forgive Baki," said the second man to step into the hall. "He frets overly for our fair province."

"It's true," added the third.

Amony put up his hand. "Gentlemen, I merely had a message from the Queen. I intend to hear you out, and with a tolerant ear. If you'll only give me a moment—"

"So, we convene in the corridors, today?" Hareb called as he strode toward the group.

Jayna never thought to be glad to see the thin, wily man.

"Your Highnesses." Hareb bowed toward Amony and Jayna before glancing at the others. "Gentlemen."

Amony nodded. "Hareb."

The chamberlain turned his attention to Jayna. "We've yet to meet this morning, and a busy day it should prove to be." He glanced at the Pharaoh. "A section of buildings on the west side of the village has collapsed. I'm sad to say, they were fully occupied at the time."

Jayna gasped. "How horrible!"

"Indeed," Hareb drawled. "Medical help is on its way, but the need is great for food and alternate shelter and such."

All eyes turned to Jayna. Obviously this was a matter for the queen.

She accepted it gladly. "Excuse me," she said, stepping away from Amony. "Perhaps we can speak later."

Her husband nodded. Behind his reserved demeanor, she could see his curiosity for what she'd wanted to say to him. She'd think up something later, or tell him the matter took care of itself.

"Good-day, Your Highness," the men bowed together.

"Good-day," Jayna returned.

A deep sigh escaped her as she hurried down the corridor, intent on summoning her ladies. She'd enlist their help in gathering whatever supplies they'd need.

She realized she wasn't alone. Hareb followed close beside her. "Is there something else you wish to discuss, Hareb?"

"I just wanted to let you know that I spoke with the Chief of Security. He's investigated the matter in the valley and determined no harmful intent in the slipping of the brick that nudged our Pharaoh."

"Is that so?" Jayna asked with barely veiled sarcasm.

Hareb smiled. "It's so. It was just an accident."

"Thank you for the news, Hareb." She smiled tartly. "I'll see you later, hmm?" With that she quickened her pace and turned down the corridor toward her chamber.

Mamo slouched a few feet beyond her door. "Mamo," she called. "Would you like to help? There's a problem in the village, and we'll need some extra hands."

The man-child hurried to his feet.

"Come with me, if you'd like." She continued on past her door with Mamo bounding along behind her. "I've got to collect my ladies first."

Jayna journeyed with the women, Mamo, and a crew of servants to the site of the buildings that had crumbled. The servants handed out dishes of food, pallets for sleeping, and new tunics to replace those not yet unearthed beneath the brick. Jayna and her ladies spoke with the people, hearing their needs for workers to help with reconstruction, and inspected the makeshift tents that housed the few victims injured in the collapse.

Returning past the dinner hour, she learned that Amony's business had prevented him, too, from attending the public dinner. She accepted a platter which she took to her chamber. Weary from her trying day in the wreckage, she ate slowly, then collapsed on her bed for a deep, thankfully dreamless sleep.

***

The first rays of the morning sun poked through her high window and woke her. Opening her eyes to a chamber glowing with yellow light, she gave silent thanks that yesterday had passed with her secret still intact. Where would she be this beautiful morning if she'd told Amony what she knew? On her way to a traitor's violent death?

Or back to the tomb?

She frowned at the dust motes that danced in the wide ray of sunshine. Why did the thought of returning to the tomb chill her as much as the thought of facing death?

She rolled over and stared at the far wall.

The answers to her fate would come eventually.

In the meantime, the Pharaoh would have to learn to love his wife enough to forgive her for what she had to say to him. His wife, in return, would have to believe in him, and trust him, before Jayna could speak.

And if that day never came?

She thought of Amony's charming rescue of her on the stair, his teasing on the terrace, and his warm arms drawing her close for a kiss on the floor of his chamber. Then she thought of the love that radiated from sister to brother as they sat arm-in-arm on a rooftop watching the sunset.

If "that day" never came, she pitied both king and queen for their lost potential.

Chapter Ten

Over the next two days, Jayna's only opportunity to spend time with Amony—and try to soften him toward her so she might warn him of the future—revolved around the walk to and from the dining room. She met him outside his chamber two nights in a row, surprising him no end. They merely talked of their day before they reached the dining room, then parted in the usual custom. Those few short minutes presented no help in the spilling of her secret. She watched Amony, and occasionally found his dark gaze on her. The yearning to speak to him was almost unbearable by the time the night was finished. Yet, frustrated by their lack of communication, she found she could barely string two words together. She took little comfort that Amony didn't press her to join him in his chamber, since her entrance into his lair appeared to be the only thing, thus far, to garner a warming of his cold manner.

At night she dreamed of Egypt. Oars slicing through the muddy waters of the Nile, farmers harvesting their fields, young girls walking along the street with their nanny. The queen's subconscious worked actively while Jayna slept, and left her feeling, each morning, as if she'd spent the night reading the woman's diary. Her dreams were too vivid and detailed to be anything less than the woman's memories coming to the fore, and Jayna became more and more aware of the woman inside her. The woman she was inside of.

The third dining, the night before the dreaded trip along the Nile, brought more of the same. Amony left her at her table and went to join the men. She sat with several nobles' wives and her newly-acquired friend, Kessie. New at court, Kessie was a welcome addition, as far as Jayna was concerned. With her sweetness, she drew the kinder and less self-serving of the noblewomen, though with the queen's stamp of approval on her, even those other types sought out her company.

This night, however, Jayna felt her soul beyond the soothing presence of gentle company. Amony sat at a table twenty feet away from her, talking with the other men, as usual. He was feeling better. The slight weight she'd felt upon her arm when walking had been non-existent tonight. She'd been aware of his strong forearm linked with hers as he walked, self-assured and powerful, alongside her. On his arm she'd felt as slight and airy as her filmy gown. He was himself again.

His gaze met hers and she looked away. Plucking a fruit from the tray, she glanced around at the women and tried to catch the flow of the conversation she'd missed.

Kessie smiled at her, noticing the return of her attention.

Jayna followed the topic for a few minutes, then glanced at Amony again. Someone at his table said something amusing, for his lips lifted in a grin that lit his handsome face. He reached out to pick up his goblet, then raised the vessel to his lips. Thick muscle rippled and sighed beneath red-brown skin.

Her hands had been on that supple flesh, her body pressed to that mighty strength.

Desire swept through Jayna.

Their moment in his chamber came back to her with a vengeance, the feel of his arms pulling her down upon him, the heated passion in his dark eyes as he'd gazed at his wife. The memory sent a shiver through her body.

She looked away.

The pressure of enduring his presence, so near and yet so far away, was almost unbearable. She had to believe the ancients had the right idea, separating lovers like this.

Lovers.

She drew in a deep breath.

We're not lovers.

She looked to Amony again.

And *he* was no killer. He couldn't have deliberately killed her brother—*the queen's brother*, she corrected. He wasn't the cold-blooded type to pursue such an action. He wasn't. He couldn't be!

Time, she thought. *Time is the key.*

If she could keep from killing Amony—an easy goal—and keep the others from killing him—a bit riskier a task—maybe the queen would have time, albeit through Jayna, to earn a place in her husband's heart that might see her through this unscathed.

Would the queen within her rebel? Would the horrible dream return to haunt her?

No matter. She had to try.

Amony's dark gaze met hers from across the crowded room. Wrapped in her thoughts, she hadn't time to avoid it. He'd caught her looking.

And she'd caught him. Their gazes locked, and this time, neither retreated before the other.

Amony stood. Jayna saw her cue and rose also. A host of guards and ladies followed suit.

Walking over to Amony, Jayna took his arm. They made their farewells to the gathering, and traversed the corridors as they had every night, except tonight the tension she felt seemed to be in him as well.

"You're better, I think," she said.

"A fact you hate?"

His question didn't sound convincing. Jayna kept her eyes averted. Had he noticed it, too, this thing between them, tonight?

He walked nearer, his arm brushing hers. His warm breath stirred her hair. "Come to my chamber with me."

Jayna's heart fluttered. She knew what he intended. Did the queen within her recoil, or was it her own virginal instinct?

"I can't."

Something within her cried out as she spoke. Was it in her eyes? Her green eyes? Could he see, in his queen's eyes, how much she wanted to come with him?

"I'm still quite weak," he said. "Not near as well as I might seem."

She couldn't help smiling at his play. "I'm not afraid of you."

"Then why won't you come?"

She released his arm. "I can't."

"Why?" The entire entourage halted as Amony followed her the few feet she'd strayed.

Her heart beat ferociously in her chest to find the queen's husband stalking her, halting her against the wall. He placed his thick, right arm beside her, cutting off her view of their followers.

"I'm not ready!" she bit the cry back to a desperate whisper. "*You're* not ready."

"I'm ready, Jayna."

The impassioned utterance tore through her soul.

"I'm not!" she said.

Amony leaned closer. "Come talk to me, then. Just come in to talk."

Passion warmed the brown eyes.

"No!" He didn't mean it. Or if he did, he wouldn't stand by it. The queen's body would be lost to him. And so would Jayna's heart be lost. "I'm tired," she breathed.

"So am I," he said. "My injury pains me—"

"Shall I send for Atep?"

"Please," he groaned. "I hope to move beyond the palace gates tomorrow. A call to him could end my intentions and doom me to my four walls."

The tumult of Jayna's emotions stalled and abruptly died at his enlightening comment. Was it true? Could Atep keep Amony from going on the trip tomorrow?

If she got word to the healer that the Pharaoh had difficulty walking tonight, he might limit Amony to the palace. She could tell him that Amony would deny it, but that she'd felt it. It was worth a shot!

"Shall you walk me to my chamber?" he asked softly.

"So that you can walk me back?"

He nodded. "Later."

"I think I'll go to my room now."

They angled toward her door. The guard and ladies hung back.

Jayna stopped, her hand on the doorframe, and turned to the king. "Good-night. I hope you feel better soon."

Amony stepped close, gathering her hand in his. "That looks likely not to happen."

Jayna's heart picked up tempo. Amony's face was so close to hers, his firm lips so near. His gaze moved softly over her face, his eyes a deep reddish-brown—hazy and warm. He leaned close, his breath gently touching her lips.

The guard couldn't know it. The ladies couldn't know it. But Jayna did. His lips touched gently upon her cheek, a soft whisper, the touch of a butterfly, but with the impact of a lightning bolt.

He turned around, leaving Jayna stunned and breathless as she watched him walk away.

Chapter Eleven

"I said we wouldn't be ready," Penda fussed as she shoved three pairs of sandals into a leather bag. "Now we've got the Pharaoh waiting on us, and for what? Oh, goodness," she tittered. "I'm dizzy with the rush."

"Let me get that." Naja brushed the older woman away from the trunk and placed a stack of gowns inside it.

Jayna sat on the high stool, unhappily watching the ladies buzz around the room while Maisha put the finishing touches of kohl on Jayna's eyes. The chaos was all her fault, of course.

She'd summoned Atep last night, told him how the Pharaoh had limped and groaned and nearly swooned. She'd thought she'd convinced him. Certain the trip would be canceled at least for this day, she'd stalled her ladies and resisted their attempts to start packing.

Amony, nevertheless, had showed at her door only minutes before, asking to escort her to the ship.

Thanks to her ladies' efficient efforts, her baggage was quickly packed and sent ahead. Jayna, accompanied by both her makeup woman and Penda, arrived breathless on the dock after not too lengthy a delay.

The host of nobles who were accompanying them didn't dare board the ship until the Pharaoh did, but the Pharaoh awaited his wife.

The regal man stood at the fore of the restless crowd, and the sight of him nearly took Jayna's breath away. Pride burgeoned in her heart to be attended by this man.

He stood with his sandaled feet spread wide, his arms crossed just beneath a sloping, turquoise necklace that lay upon his stalwart chest. As was typical, a white linen kilt cinched his narrow waist. The lack of wig, headdress, and armbands signaled this outing as the pleasure trip it was intended.

Avoiding the watchful eyes of Tiy, Sefu, Roble, Rana and Desta, Jayna walked straight to Amony. Their gazes bore into her, nonetheless, as she smiled at her husband. A small smile. The queen could offer him little else. The people who hated him and wanted him dead would accept the sight of nothing more.

Amony nodded, his gaze moving warmly over her face. "My Queen." He presented his arm and she laid her hand upon it. His heated skin suffused her with a warmth that went beyond the simple heat of the day. His white teeth flashed in a smile. Did he feel it, too?

He turned his attention to the crowd of nobles. "Shall we board?"

The group quickly fell in step behind the royal couple. Amony led Jayna to the golden ship waiting in the water. A tall mast stood proud, eager to unfurl its sail in the wind. The passengers crossed the deck and took up positions, either standing at the tall sides of the ship or seated on the plush lounges arranged fore and aft of the sail.

Amony drew Jayna to the stern. Captain and crew got the ship moving.

Sefu wasted little time in approaching them. "A better day to be alive, I couldn't name. How's our Pharaoh feeling on the matter?"

As if on cue, Roble appeared at their other side and laid his hand on Amony's back. "Your Highness."

So soon? Jayna's legs turned to jelly as she recalled the description of the push Roble had gloated over at their meeting. The palace had only just disappeared from sight. Wouldn't the group wait until the ship moved farther along the Nile?

"Your Grace." The sound of a friendly voice sapped Jayna's strength with the force of her relief. Her breath escaped her in a pant as she looked at the newcomer, Nassor. Sefu and Roble couldn't harm Amony with another this close. While the other men conversed, she smiled at the court flirt.

"Your eyes are so glum," the handsome man said. "Be of cheer. This trip is just what everyone needs. You'll adore the place. Trees everywhere. Wildlife. Very refreshing after the city life. I don't recommend it for every day, but as a holiday? Definitely."

Jayna glanced at Sefu and Roble. They seemed unconcerned that Nassor had joined them. Was it only an act? Should she make the appearance of trying to get rid of him? How could she do that if his presence might be the only thing keeping Amony from receiving a blow to the back of his head?

She turned toward the water, keeping half an eye on both Amony and Nassor. If Sefu and Roble were listening, she'd have to say the right thing to make Nassor go away. But she had to keep Nassor from believing it and doing that very thing.

"I'm not the greatest company, right now," she said. Turning toward the man, she said softly, "This trip is not all pleasure, for me."

"Why not?" he asked.

Casting a careful glance at the other men, she gazed back at the waters of the Nile. "Life is just not so easy that I can break away and forget everything. Even for a moment."

Nassor leaned close. "The royal life," he said softly. He looked deliberately at the king's back. "Would you like to take a stroll?"

The man had suggested before, in Amony's chamber, that she and Amony weren't getting along. Jayna didn't know why, but she hated that. She would set him straight.

"We aren't as—"

"Your Highness." A gentleman Jayna had only recently discovered as a distant great-uncle of Amony's stopped beside her and bowed. His gaze lifted to his nephew. "Amony."

Jayna welcomed the sight of the man more than she had Nassor. The group could harangue her all they wanted. When family came to call, there was no stopping them.

The five of them were drawn for some time into Manu's extroverted personality. When the talk turned to wartime strategies, Sefu looked beleaguered but resigned. Relief soared through Jayna. If Sefu couldn't get the man away, she certainly had no hope of doing so. Nassor massaged her shoulder. "How about that stroll?"

Jayna still didn't want to leave Amony. There was no telling when Manu would tire and move on, or if Sefu would be sufficiently clever in distracting him. Roble excused himself and took a seat that afforded a decent view of them, but he eyed the older man's back as if plotting just how he could lure the man away.

"I enjoy the view from here," she told Nassor. "You may roam about, if you wish." To be safe, she favored him with a regretful look. Should Manu be successfully removed, perhaps she might still have Nassor to fall back on.

A young girl of no more than six came running across the deck. Her mother chased her, calling her. "Efia, get back here. Efia!" At the sight of her little girl charging full force into the Pharaoh's legs, she groaned. "Your Highness, I'm so sorry. Efia!"

Amony boosted the child in the air. Her tiny feet dangled as the two looked into one another's eyes.

"What are you up to, little one?" Amony asked gently, curtailing his discussion with his uncle.

Big, bright eyes widened further. "I wanted to walk about."

"Your mama doesn't want you to?"

The little girl shook her head. "She said I'd get in the way, but I just wanted to see the people, and the river, and—" her gaze darted toward Jayna "—the Queen."

A slow smile stole over Amony's face. "She's very pretty, isn't she?"

Jayna's heart gave a twist.

The little girl nodded.

Amony settled the child in the crook of his arm. "It just so happens that I was about to take the Queen for a walk, to look at the river and the people. Shall we ask your mama if you can join us?"

Efia nodded again.

Amony looked to the distraught mother who appeared to relax immeasurably. She even smiled. "Are you certain, Your Highness? She's a handful."

"We'll be fine." His warm gaze met Jayna's. "The Queen will help me."

The woman nodded. "Thank you."

"We'll bring her back shortly." Amony held his free arm out to Jayna. "My Queen?"

Jayna placed her hand on his warm skin. Tearing her gaze away from the Pharaoh's mesmerizing red-brown eyes, she looked to the little girl who stared back at her with awe.

"Hello, Efia," Jayna said gently.

"Your Highness," came the tiny reply.

"We're a couple of lucky girls to get to walk with the Pharaoh, aren't we?"

Efia nodded, and beamed a smile.

Above the child's head, Amony's gaze rested on her. He watched her, as if measuring her words.

At last he looked down at the little girl. "Do you see the man, there, with the green tunic? He's standing by the lady in yellow. Do you know what his tunic is made of? Crocodile skin." The little girl's eyes grew wide. "He wrestled the beastie just outside his back door. He's got sandals and a nice bag, too, for his efforts."

The girl laughed. "No, he didn't."

"He did," Amony insisted. "Ask him. I'll take you over." His arm moved, his hand slipping to Jayna's. Their fingers linked, and he glanced at her.

She smiled.

It's okay, her smile told him.

The king and queen needed this tenderness.

An answering smile touched Amony's lips as he secured her hand more fully in his own.

Despite her thoughts of helping the queen, a warm flush spread over Jayna's cheeks. The physical chemistry between the royal couple was more than she could manage. If the queen hadn't yet discovered this sizzle between them, she was certainly experiencing it now.

Amony guided them toward the man. "Safi, tell little Efia where you got your tunic."

Safi launched into a rather comedic version of his confrontation with the crocodile, delighting the little girl and Jayna as well. When he was done, he allowed them to touch the edge of his tunic, then produced the crocodile bag for their amazed inspection.

The threesome moved on to the rail of the boat to watch the shoreline for a glimpse of one of the dangerous reptiles. Efia squealed in pleasure and a little trepidation at seeing a pair of crocodiles creep up a far bank.

They returned the child to her mother some time later. Jayna enjoyed the respite. No one had come near during the tour with the child, so she'd had little to fear. Roble and his wife, Rana, were quick to join them as soon as the child was gone. As a married couple with three small children at home with their nurses, they had a pleasant opening to approach the king. Jayna shuddered to think that this couple, speaking so fondly of their children, might be the very ones to end Amony's life.

She caught the eye of a nobleman she knew to be loyal to Amony and tipped her head with a subtle smile. She looked away, then back again. He watched her. She glanced around to see if the gesture had been witnessed. It hadn't. She smiled again, warmly, and the man rose and came to her.

"How are you, Neru?" she cried as if he'd come upon them unawares. "Are you enjoying the trip?"

She didn't know the man very well, but she'd make all the small talk she could think of to keep him at Amony's side.

***

At last, Bene's whitewashed villa came into view beyond the shoreline. Their host and hostess met the party, and Jayna got a reprieve as Bene claimed the Pharaoh's company.

Within the hour, however, her peace fled. Bene knew nothing of the plot. A moment of distraction, and the others could do their evil work. She tried to steer her hostess close to Amony's group, but far too many snatches of time were lost from her. Each time, she thought she wouldn't see Amony again. Visions assailed her of Hareb or Roble running from the direction of the stables, or through the doors of the estate, crying "The Pharaoh is dead! The Pharaoh is dead!"

As the sun traveled lower in the sky, the entire retinue assembled for a fine dinner out on the terrace. Lush green grounds sprawled around them, and a tranquil pool glistened, devoid of the flowering lotus, for it had been stocked with fish to entertain those who might be inclined toward a little sport on the morrow.

Amony sat with the master of the estate, his back to the open yard. For the moment, he was safe. Jayna ate only sparingly, then wandered out into the yard, out of sight of the diners. Coming across a fallen tree on the outskirts of the green, she sat down and buried her face in her hands. Keeping

Amony alive exhausted her. He might have died ten times over this very day. The sight of Roble's hand upon the Pharaoh's back not once, but twice, lingered with her.

She massaged her closed eyelids, and could barely control the shaking that seized her fingers. Her entire body trembled, and for the first time, she truly longed to awaken in the cold tomb.

A warm leg brushed against hers, and a gentle hand caressed her back. She needed the soothing—her body responded instantly—but too many back-stabbers appeared to have warm hands. She looked up quickly.

Of all the people she might have imagined to come and comfort her in this moment, Amony wasn't one of them.

He sat next to her and continued to caress her back, his dark eyes soft. "The day grows heavy on you?"

Jayna's heart pulsed with tenderness for the man as she savored the warm touch of his hand through her gown. His fingers brushed the skin above her neckline, sending a tingle of excitement through her. Could the queen feel it, too?

She expelled a tense breath, then smiled. "It grows better by the moment."

Amony's brow arched in surprise, and the strong hand ceased its movement. "Would Her Highness like to take a tour of the river?"

Nothing sounded nicer than spending time alone with Amony in this beauty.

She looked around. Plenty of guileless witnesses had finished their dinners and come to roam the green.

A private walk, however, might carry the royals directly into an ambush. Or be met with the expectation that Jayna, herself, not return with the king.

"Let's stay here," she said.

Amony appeared to expect that, but if she'd disappointed him, he didn't show it. He nodded.

***

Tiy approached her that night. "What an unlucky day. Such cloying companions I've never met. Sefu has come up with a plan, though. Even now, he's got our host by the ears, and by the time he's done with him, there will be a hunt on the morrow. Of course, only our loyal supporters will take part. And Amony. He won't be able to squirm out of this trap, and we'll have witnesses aplenty."

"What sort of hunt?"

"Hippopotami, alligator...anything capable of eating a king, my dear." She chuckled. "If the wildlife won't accommodate the men, the men will accommodate the wildlife. An unconscious meal should be just as tasty as a struggling one, maybe more so." She shrugged. "His body will never be found, I'm sure, and with the witnesses to testify that he'll never be back..."

Jayna paced her chamber once Tiy was gone. She had to do something. Amony couldn't go out with those men tomorrow, even if one of his faithful went along. One moment with his ally's head turned, and the others could send Amony to his doom.

She instructed a servant to call on her when Amony retired to his quarters. Nearly an hour passed before the servant knocked. Without further delay, she stepped out into the corridor and hurried the few feet to his rooms.

He looked surprised to see her.

"Your Highness." He gave a slight bow. "To what or whom do I owe this honor?"

After all her waiting and worrying, she didn't hesitate. "I wondered if you'd be free tomorrow for that turn by the river. That is, if your hip is well enough for such a venture."

"My hip is well enough." He stared at her for a long moment. "You've heard, of course, that a hunt has been organized, and I'll be away for the day."

"I heard about the hunt," she said. "But—"

"You suddenly can't bear to be parted from me?" He smiled ruefully. "You come to me with an offer I've already made to you because you know I can't accept."

"No!" she said. "I just—hoped, thought—you might be—interested."

"I'm interested."

"Then we'll do it?" she asked, encouraged.

"I can't." He raised a hand and gently stroked her face. The contact sent a jolt through her, but his expression belied his tenderness. The dark eyes mocked her. "I hope you're not too disappointed."

"I am disappointed," she said. "I'm very disappointed."

"Why?" he asked.

"Because I want to do this."

"Why?" The dark eyes watched her closely.

"Because I've thought about your earlier offer, and I know I'll regret missing it, once we return." Truth stole its way from her tongue. "It's a memory I wish to have."

"The two of us walking by the river?" His mouth twisted wryly. "Then we'll do it when I return."

"It'll surely be dark."

"You still fear the night," he observed. "Or is it the combination of your husband and the night?"

"I fear the sun," she said, before she thought.

He looked truly shocked now, and she realized the ramifications of what she'd said. As Pharaoh, Amony worshipped the sun-god.

"You fear life, itself, Your Majesty?"

Jayna moistened her lips and pressed on in desperation. "Yes. This life we live frightens me. King and Queen have never known such distance. My heart has never known such distance from my head."

He frowned. "What are you saying?"

Reaching out, she grasped both his hands in hers. "Stay with me tomorrow. Let's walk the river. Or swim. Or fish.

Everyone's been telling me how much fun it's going to be. Stay with me. My day is yours, the whole day. I promise. Let the others go without you, and you won't regret it."

"They'll cancel, anyway, rather than leave me behind."

She squeezed his hands. "Don't let them cancel. They'll only interfere with our time if they stay."

A smile twisted the corner of Amony's lips.

"I'm serious," she said. "That whole group is all business." And she was serious on that. "Send them on. Insist. Or back out at the last moment. Something. Let tomorrow be a day of leisure."

"Today was busy," he said, thoughtful.

"It was," she agreed.

"I had barely a moment alone."

Warmth flushed Jayna's face. Did he mean something by that? Had he noticed how desperately she'd fought to keep him in good company? Plentiful company?

Her company?

Chapter Twelve

When Amony stepped back off the boat and waved the others on, Jayna glanced the twenty-odd yards distant to where Tiy and Desta stood watching. Though her heart soared, she adopted a confused frown for their benefit as Amony walked toward her.

"What are you doing, Your Highness?" Though the women couldn't hear her every word, she went through the motions, hoping Amony would see her game. "Aren't you going on the hunt?"

"No, My Queen," the Pharaoh replied lightly. "I'm going to spend the day with you. The whole day. What do you think of that?"

Jayna could have kissed him for playing along so perfectly. Her sport with him pleased her far beyond the more deadly ruse posed by Tiy and Desta.

She arched her eyebrows as if surprised. "If you're certain you wouldn't enjoy yourself more on the hunt."

"I'm certain of it." A smile touched Amony's firm mouth. "You see, I've been promised a day I won't regret."

So he remembered that? Why did the words sound so much more provocative coming from his handsome lips? She looked away from the mesmerizing man. She had to get through this moment with Tiy and Desta convinced she'd had nothing to do with Amony's abrupt change of plans.

She heaved a sigh, hoping the curious women took full note of the despondency with which she shrugged her shoulders. "What do you have in mind that we should do?"

Amony's gaze dipped for the briefest of seconds, making her acutely aware of her low bodice, but he responded easily with the plan she'd given him. "Fish, perhaps. Join in the swimming, when it begins. Then, maybe—" his white teeth flashed in a grin "—a walk by the river?"

Jayna couldn't restrain her smile. She bowed her head, letting her hair sweep down alongside her face to shield her pleasure from prying eyes. Pressing her lips together, she composed a calm expression, then met Amony's gaze again.

His charming smile remained in place. "Shall we approach our hostess for fishing poles?"

***

"Hold still." Amony stood at the edge of the pool, their tangled lines threaded through his fingers. Jayna held both their poles tightly. The Pharaoh pulled the lines from the water, then twisted toward her. "We got one!"

At the end of the jumble of line squirmed a rambunctious, pale-blue fish. Just whose line had snagged it was anyone's guess. The thrashing fish performed a wild flip over Amony's wrist, cinching the line tight. Amony raised his arm and stared at the spectacle with wide eyes. He met Jayna's gaze, then stretched his arm forward. "A bracelet for my lady?"

His jest caught her off-guard, so unexpected and wonderfully apt it was. She burst into giggles.

"I rather fancy this one," he said, seemingly unaware of her amusement, "but I can make another. Maybe a smaller one for you—ouch!" He trapped the squirming fish in his palm. "A less scaly one, too."

Jayna laughed in delight at the regal king and his lively bracelet until she caught sight of heads turning their way. She and Amony had their own little spot at the pool, but they were far from alone. Plenty of other fishermen, and fisherwomen—notably Tiy and Desta—were in attendance.

She cleared her throat and squelched her cheer. Amony freed his aquatic trinket, tossed it back into the water, then calmly untangled the lines.

The fishing didn't last much longer. After snagging her line with Amony's a third time, Jayna could no longer hide her pleasure with the king's charming manner and amusing antics. Tiy and Desta watched too closely.

She suggested a change of sport, and Amony gathered up their gear. He signaled a servant who promptly rushed forward with a reed basket.

"It's near time for our noon meal, anyway," he said. "Our hostess has arranged a bite for us."

As he traded burdens with the servant, Jayna pondered what might have pre-disposed the woman to such an action. She could only conclude that Amony had requested it.

"That was thoughtful of her," she said when he turned, the basket slung over his arm.

His slow smile answered hers.

"Where shall we go?" she asked.

Her escort glanced around, thoughtful. Jayna watched the sun's rays catch his eyes, highlighting the translucent, reddish-brown of his irises. Her heart gave a painful tug. He was so incredibly handsome, with his changeable eyes and night-black hair. Had the queen never seen this? Had she never felt anything for him but hate?

"The river?" Amony's gaze returned to her. "We can have our meal, and our walk."

"Do you know your way about?"

Amony tipped his head, and they began walking toward the woodline. "I know enough that we won't require a search party to bring us back out."

Within moments of entering the forest, Jayna forgot the sprawling, flat green they'd left behind. Vines hung from tall trees, and the buzz of insects filled her ears, then intensified. "Are there snakes out here?" she asked, worried.

"Stay near me."

She frowned at Amony. "Do you have a weapon of some sort?"

"A knife."

"Do you think you'll be using it?" Her voice thinned and wavered at the end of her question.

Surprise stamped Amony's features. "You're really afraid, aren't you?"

Jayna nodded.

"I'm sorry." He pulled her to his side, his arm around her shoulders. "We're almost there."

"Where?"

"You'll see."

"Hmm. Secret—" A loud croak from something in the weeds near her feet made her jump.

Amony tightened his arm around her, and when she calmed, she noticed a satisfied grin played about his lips.

"Did you stage this to terrify me?"

He gazed down his noble nose at her. "That you might cling to my side? Of course." He gave a soft laugh.

She smiled, comfortable in the circle of his arm. If he had planned this trek for its fright quality, he was a genius. The queen wasn't at all afraid of his manly body when lord-knew what manner of snakes and other wildlife might leap out at her, or drop from the treetops. In fact, being this close to him was quite pleasant. His firm body pleasured her bare arms, his manly, exotic scent teased her nostrils.

"Here it is," he announced.

They stepped out of the trees and into a glade.

Jayna's smile froze and faded, though she scarcely realized it.

An ocean of blue, violet, lilac and lavender shifted beneath her stunned gaze. Only a hint of green could be seen in a field teeming with larkspur so tall in some places that it surely reached six feet in height. The loose spikes of the flowers fluttered in the breeze, sending their sweet aroma flooding through her senses.

The flowers from her wedding. Her wedding to Amony.

Memory rocked Jayna. Her mind spun, and she fought to stay erect.

The flowers had been everywhere. Secured in bunches to the chairs of their guests. On her veil.

She could see it. The flowers. The sun. Him.

He was perfect. Perfect and hated. Like a moth drawn to flame, she'd darted around him. Or was it he around her?

She closed her eyes, and her heart swelled with...affection? Tenderness? *Love?*

It couldn't be!

Her eyelids flew open.

Was she feeling the queen's wishes for her wedding, or the reality?

Amony's face swam before her shrinking vision. The queen had beheld beauty, her heart twisted with...doubt?

Did she doubt Amony's guilt?

Did she have reservations about the role she undertook as Amony's killer?

Yes.

Jayna blinked.

Yes!

The field of larkspur waved silently, retreating from what it had been to what it was. A field of flowers.

She looked at Amony.

Guilt and pain flickered across his face before he looked away. He'd watched her reaction to seeing the field. Had he meant to remind her of their wedding day?

He knew he had reminded her.

She reached out and took his hand.

His startled gaze returned to her, and she smiled.

Memory rushed over her, as smooth and welcoming as silk. Amony wasn't a killer, anymore than she was a killer. All the anger, all the outrage, all the grief, couldn't bring back the queen's brother. She had to go on, and she'd known it. Not with the enemy. No. But Amony was not that man. She'd seen evil, and Amony wasn't of that spirit.

By the time they'd wed, the queen hadn't believed her husband capable of murder.

***

The royal couple returned as the sky lost its last red-gold ray of sun. Amony walked Jayna to her door.

"You made good on your promise," he said. "I've never had a better day."

Jayna leaned back against the wall and sighed. "Neither have I."

Amony's gaze caressed her. "I almost hate to leave tomorrow. This place is charmed."

She shook her head. "It's not this place."

For once, she didn't retreat beneath the heat that flamed in his eyes. Not even when his gaze moved to her mouth.

Her heart drummed at a steady pace with a need she wouldn't deny. She wanted his kiss. The queen wanted his kiss. The flighty panic of a virgin-child would gain her nothing.

His thick arm reached toward her, and her skin came alive as his warm hand cupped her waist. Silkily, his arm wound around her back, bringing her body closer to his. He stretched his other hand up to her face, his gaze moving across her features while his palm caressed her cheek.

Jayna struggled to keep her eyes aloft, but his touch inflamed her and drove her mad for the feel of his lips on hers. Just a taste. Just a touch. The queen needed it.

She reached out to him, her world spinning as her aching hands met his bare flesh.

His mouth claimed hers. Wave after shocking wave raced through her, chased by the full, moist pressure of his mouth. Never had she felt so completely swept outside herself, so—

—fulfilled. She'd wanted this for so long. His kiss. His passionate lips moving against hers, slanting, taking, giving. His strong arms wrapped around her, pressing her against his firm chest.

Far too soon, his lips left her.

Jayna couldn't meet his gaze. Did he know? Had he felt what she felt? The queen's presence?

She took a dizzying step back from his heated body. Coherent thought eluded her, and when she opened her mouth to speak, she couldn't form a sound. She had to go. Twisting, she pushed through her door and shoved it closed behind her.

"He kissed you."

Jayna gasped at the sight of Tiy and Desta standing, frowning, just inside her room.

"I know that look," Tiy said. The lines between her brows carved deeply. "Don't try to deny it. Ohh, this is dangerous ground. Next, you'll be in his bed."

Desta nodded. "It's happening, and you don't even know it."

"That's how it works," Tiy said gravely. "A kiss here, a caress there, then you're in bed and in love."

Desta put her arm around Jayna's shoulders. "We don't blame you. You're young. You've never experienced this sort of thing."

Tiy, too, stepped close to Jayna. "You need to take a lover to fulfill your needs."

"How about Nassor?" Desta asked. Her gaze moved carefully to Tiy.

The older woman nodded her approval. "He's more than a little attracted to our queen, from what I can see. He'd make a perfect lover."

Jayna's mind spun. How did they know Amony had kissed her? Could she deny it? She pushed a hand through her hair, the memory of the queen's need rushing through her. *Nassor. They wanted her to take Nassor as a lover.* "I don't know..."

"I insist," Tiy said. Desta dropped her arm from Jayna's shoulders and wandered a few paces away while Tiy spoke to her. "You have to put Amony off. He's a determined man. He'll have you before you know it's happened."

Jayna shook her head and tried to make her voice light. "It's not so serious."

"You're married," Tiy said firmly. "Only your coldness thus far has kept him from you. Just the memory of today's tender smile may see you bedded down."

"It may be too late," Desta warned from afar, proving she had heard their every word.

Tiy gripped Jayna's shoulders. "Tomorrow you must find an escort and don't let him leave your side. I don't want to bring the others into this. Intimacies made into group-discussion could prove extremely dangerous for you." Her eyes glittered with meaning. "Do as I say. Protect yourself, and we'll keep it among the three of us. Do you understand?"

Jayna nodded, afraid she understood only too well.

Tiy had just threatened her.

Chapter Thirteen

That night, vivid dreams of her brother came to her again. These were gentle dreams, though. She and Daren playing in the sand. Daren heading out on duty, his face proud as he manned his chariot, a bright helm covering his dark hair. He waved, his gaze touching her as he smiled. "Take care, little sister."

And his return, watching the sun set in blinding shades of orange from the flat rooftop of their house. The wind blew gently through their hair as they sat, shoulder to shoulder, speaking of—

Jayna awoke with a start.

They'd spoken only in whispers, so their parents wouldn't hear. Daren had...what? Mother and Father couldn't know.

Jayna closed her eyes and held herself very still. The moments ticked by.

Whatever it was, their parents would be upset to know. Thus the whispering. The secrecy.

She couldn't remember. She couldn't grasp it.

She lunged from the bed.

Fresh air beckoned from the terrace. She stepped out into the night air and drew in deep, cleansing breaths.

Two memories were rapidly meshing in her mind. Two realities. The queen had never been so present and alive inside her. Jayna had felt the need, that first night, to look for the woman, to call out for her. That need no longer existed. The queen dwelled inside her as assuredly as she dwelled inside the queen.

Strangely, the knowledge didn't threaten her, or feel foreign in any way. Every nuance of the queen, every memory, whether fleeting or full, made her feel as if she were simply being reminded of something she'd forgotten.

Closing her eyes, Jayna savored the peace that flooded through her.

***

"The Pharaoh is here to escort you to the ship."

Her husband had come for her, and she had to reject him. Jayna hadn't forgotten Tiy's warning.

What would Amony think? Hopefully only that she was a slow riser. She wanted to run to the door, fling it open and throw her arms around him. Instead, she said, "Tell him we'll meet him there."

After a minute, Penda came back into the room.

"What did he say?" Jayna asked.

"Nothing."

"How did he look? Did he look—upset?"

"He looked firm."

Jayna released a sigh. She had no idea what he would construe the rejection of his escort to mean, but she feared that he'd take it for the worst. Her heart ached with the suspicion that the worst had to come at any rate. As long as Tiy and Desta were near, she'd have to avoid, even reject, Amony. The trip back down the river promised to be torture.

They left the chamber a few minutes later.

Nassor met them outside. "Your Highness," he beamed. "Tiy gave me your message. I couldn't be happier to accompany you on our return."

They walked toward the river. The entire entourage stood on shore sharing last minute conversation with their hosts. Jayna couldn't look Amony in the eye as they neared for fear of seeing the betrayal she felt in her own heart. She joined in offering her thanks to her hosts, then turned with the rest to board the ship.

"Beautiful estate," Nassor said from her side. "I'd almost forgotten the pleasures of the city. Of course, then I came to my senses."

His laughter coincided with the steel-tight band that clamped around her wrist. Turning, Jayna looked into her husband's dark eyes. With gentle yet unyielding pressure, he pulled her toward him. She didn't resist, nor did she feel resistance from the woman who'd sat with a brother and watched the sun set from a breezy rooftop. Satisfaction burgeoned within her. A deep relief. She need not continue along her solitary path.

The grip on her wrist loosened, and the dark eyes softened. Amony slid his hand to the small of her back and escorted her aboard the ship. He watched the last passenger embark, then nodded at the captain.

His Highness accepted no companions in their little corner near the stern, save his wife. Appearances would suggest that the Queen's arrival with Nassor had displeased the Pharaoh. Tiy's plan had backfired, and joy echoed through Jayna for her husband's firm handling of the situation.

His arm stayed around her, alternating only to hold her hand, and she tried to keep her face averted from those who watched with evil intent lest they see her pleasure. She and Amony watched the river flow and spoke quietly of their trip, the glade, and the mighty river itself.

Once, he leaned close, and she knew he wanted to kiss her. She knew it, but she couldn't let it happen. She had to make Tiy and Desta believe that other kiss was just a fluke, nothing to be repeated. Turning her face away, she'd stared out at the water.

A single thought nagged her. How could she develop a relationship with Amony, given the facade she had to present? No woman could further her love life when her lover's life depended on her rejection of him. She couldn't help thinking she was failing Amony. If she cared for him, she'd hide every tender look. She'd step out of his encircling arm instead of into it. She'd adopt the cold manner the queen had displayed from the start of her marriage.

Was that what the queen had been doing all along? Keeping distance in her marriage, so the conspirators to Amony's demise wouldn't discover her true feelings?

And why not? Hadn't Tiy just threatened her?

Without realizing it, her fingers tightened on Amony's. He looked down at her. "Something disturbs you?"

She shook her head. "It's nothing."

Then the shouts came. Crewmen dashed to the side of the ship. "We're taking on water. There's a hole in the ship! We're taking on water!"

Chapter Fourteen

Amony drew her with him, but released her hand as they neared the other passengers. "Stay with them."

"No." Jayna reached for him. "I'm coming with you."

"I have to see what the trouble is. You'll be fine with Kessie."

Jayna held his hand tight and kept her voice low. "I was thinking of you."

Her handsome husband smiled. "I'll be fine. Wait here, and I'll be back in a moment. I won't have my queen in the fray." He gave her fingers a gentle squeeze, then let go. "Now, stay here."

Jayna had heard a few of his commands, and this was one of them. She nodded, and watched him walk away.

Kessie rose to stand behind her. "The Pharaoh's ship won't sink, Your Highness."

"I know," Jayna said, not taking her eyes off Amony as the traitors, Roble and Sefu, joined the crew to peer over the side of the vessel. Was this an honest mishap, or had one of the conspirators taken matters into his or her own hands and made this mischief on the ship? They'd been so sure Amony wouldn't return alive, yet here they were, almost home.

Amony, regal and powerful, didn't suspect a thing as he inspected the hole. He leaned over the side, and Jayna held her breath. With the crewmen surrounding him, she lost sight of him. And Sefu stood so near. So near! A subtle push, and no one would see anything. The crocodiles could gulp Amony before anything could be done. A small accident gone deadly wrong for the King of Egypt.

Jayna moved slowly nearer to the side of the ship. Though a good distance from the damaged area, she was near the water. If Amony should go in, she would go in. His would be an unexpected plunge, with god-only-knew what repercussions. She would dive in after him, help him, face a hungry croc if need be. She couldn't live out the day without him. She'd come to save him, not watch him die.

After several minutes, he detached himself from the group. Tense as she could ever remember being, Jayna hurried to meet him. She clasped his arm with relief and tried to keep her voice from shaking. "Is the damage serious?"

He shook his head. "We'll be fine, but we're going to disembark while the crew see if they can get the hole sealed."

He gave the news to the concerned nobles. A host of murmurs and questions rose.

"How long will it take?"

"Is the ship going to sink?"

Amony held up his hand. "The captain and crew are quite capable. Let's get to shore and let them do their work. You might want to gather some things you'll want with you on shore. We'll have a bite to eat, then see how they've progressed."

A half hour later, the passengers sat upon a grassy bank eating honey cake and sipping wine. Jayna watched Amony converse with the crew while they inspected the hole. Shortly thereafter, he announced that the ship wouldn't be ready before dark. The party would need to travel inland to a village a small distance away to secure rest for the night.

Tiy and Sefu exchanged smug glances. Roble and Rana snuggled arm-in-arm. For a group who didn't want to return to the palace with a live king, this was a wonderful turn of events. Had they staged it? Was some other mishap awaiting Amony? Dropping the remainder of her honey cake to the ground, Jayna took a sip of her wine and nearly choked. Her throat was too tight to allow even a drop of liquid through.

A warm hand grasped her arm. She looked up into her husband's face.

He gazed at her tenderly. "We'll have to go through a bit of jungle. Not afraid, are you?"

She smiled. "Not with you at my side. Just—don't leave me, please?"

A rakish grin pulled at his mouth. "Never willingly."

She nodded. "Then don't. For any reason."

His face grew serious, and he pulled her close. "It's not so long a walk. I guarantee we'll all arrive at the village in one piece."

She believed him. He'd look out for her and the others. She would look out for him.

She nodded, and he gave her hand a gentle squeeze.

The party started off for the village, guardsmen in the lead. Some flanked the group, a few followed behind. Assessing this set-up, Jayna couldn't see any way harm could be perpetrated on Amony without a guard witnessing it. Relaxing slightly, she promptly gave her fears over to snakes and other reptilian dangers as they climbed over fallen trees and ducked low-hanging vines. The less agile of the group were just beginning to show signs of tiring when they emerged into an open field.

A village of red mud-brick homes lay before them, intersected by three streets that were little more than broad footpaths. The more pampered of the nobles groaned. "I thought we were to find shelter for the night."

"We will," Amony assured.

The villagers spotted the wealthy party approaching on foot and gathered to stare. Two took on the duty of stepping forward to greet them. "Welcome to Frena."

Amony drew Jayna to his side. "Your welcome is appreciated by the Pharaoh and his Queen."

The men's gazes darted between Jayna and Amony, over their fine clothes, then went past them to the regally dressed entourage. They dropped immediately to the ground in humble bows which their fellow townspeople imitated.

Amony continued. "Our party has lost use of our ship for the night and need shelter."

The men leaped to their feet, one saying, "It will be our honor to have Your Royal Highness and the Royal Wife in our presence. Please come. Have drink and rest."

The village was more prosperous than it appeared. None in the noble party could complain overly. Delicious wine was brought forth, fruit and meat offered. As a royal representative, Jayna felt she should stay near the king. The eyes of the group didn't tell her she erred.

While the party relaxed and took refreshment, arrangements were being made for their accommodations. Villagers kindly gave up their homes, then went quickly to friends to discuss what noble activities might go forth beneath their own roofs. The sacrifice would give them a topic of discussion for a long time to come, making them an admired center of attention.

The women in the party, including servants, broke into three groups and were assigned a like number of homes. The men did the same. The final home, the best Frena had to offer, would go to the Pharaoh and Queen, and their small handful of personal servants. Learning this, Jayna had mixed emotions. She'd never had the prospect of spending so much time in close proximity to Amony. A royal marriage was much different from anyone else's. At least, hers was. What would Tiy and Desta make of it? Should she refuse? Would the Jayna of old insist on bunking with her lady friends?

The answers to her questions were laid to rest as the two men who'd greeted their party took them on a turn of the village to locate their loaned homes. Night was fully upon them, and the men carried torches to aid the bright quarter-moon that highlighted their way. Walking alongside Amony, Jayna felt hands pulling back on her arms. She glanced sharply to each side. Tiy walked on one side of her, Rana, the other.

"Get him to come out tonight," Tiy whispered, her gaze moving to Amony's back. "Take a romantic walk beneath the stars, if need be."

"That shouldn't be too far a stretch, should it?" Rana asked, her sarcastic drawl stunning Jayna. Had Tiy told Rana what she suspected between Jayna and Amony?

"What do you mean?" she asked, fear spiraling up inside her.

"Draw him out," Rana said. "Take a walk. Wander far and long."

Tiy squeezed Jayna's arm, her fingers biting in painfully. "Do you understand?"

Jayna opened her mouth, but no words would form. They had something planned, a way to kill Amony, and she was supposed to walk him into it?

She took too long answering. Tiy's fingers dug deeper, and she asked again, her whisper fierce, "Do you understand?"

"Yes," Jayna said. She understood, and she would most definitely not do as they asked.

"Good."

The women parted. Breaking into groups, they were shown to their houses, guards accompanying them. The men and their guards parted, then the villagers showed the royal couple to their lodgings on the edge of the village.

The town's spokesman, and owner of this home, paused in the doorway. "Send one of your guards next door, should you need anything. I'll be staying there with my wife and daughters. They've readied everything here for you, and will be back in the morning to do what they can."

Jayna and Amony voiced their thanks.

The man bowed. "We're very honored by your visit and wish to do anything to make your time here pleasant."

"You're a host beyond compare," Amony praised.

"Good-night, Your Highness." The man looked to Jayna. "Your Highness."

Jayna smiled at the man, then the door shut. Save a single helpman for the king, and two ladies who would promptly leave for their small rooms at the back of the house, the king and queen were alone. Jayna drew a deep breath as Penda signaled to her from the master bedroom that she'd share with Amony.

Inside, Maisha removed Jayna's wig and makeup. Penda located her sleeping gown and helped her slip into it. Jayna found herself suddenly questioning the appropriateness of her usual nighttime apparel. It was bad enough that the material was so sheer, but the neckline plummeted deep, revealing the upper half of her breasts, and the hem fell only to mid-thigh.

"May I have my robe, please?"

Penda draped the thin material over her shoulders. Jayna drew the front corners high over her chest. "Thank you."

Wishing she could make the women stay—worse, knowing she could—she let them go. The day had been long, especially for Penda. Neither woman had fared well in their journey to the village. Penda still looked red-in-the-face from her exertions, and Maisha, beauty that she was, could barely focus on Jayna for her dismay at her own appearance.

Alone, and fearing that moment when she should no longer be, Jayna looked at the bed. Should she make use of it, or sit in the chair? She halted in indecision in the center of the room.

Draw him out, Rana had said. *Wander far and long.*

She couldn't do that. They could think anything they wanted, but she'd tell them he'd refused, that he'd been tired and fractious and not given to a stroll, no matter how she'd cajoled.

But what would best facilitate that? The bed, or the chair?

Amony strode in before she could make her decision.

He'd washed; his hair was still wet. Dressed in a fresh white kilt, he'd removed his thick necklace and gold bands from his ankles and muscular arms. She turned away and slowly meandered the room. After a few steps, she faced the wall. She had no choice but to turn. She did so slowly and met his gaze. The dark eyes watched her.

Seeking any sight but him, she glanced at the chair. Then sat.

Looking casually about the plain room, she let her gaze drift back to her husband. The dark gaze hadn't shifted from her. Her heart twisted and picked up a wild tempo.

She and the Pharaoh were truly alone for the first time in their marriage.

"You look ready to burst at the seams."

His quiet observation hit upon the truth.

"I'm restless," she blurted.

His lips curved in a slight smile.

Oh, why had she said that?

For an excuse to stay out of bed, she answered herself, but wouldn't have being tired served her better? Exhaustion would have done more.

Oh, why couldn't she claim a sudden need to walk? She'd escape this quiet torment, but Amony would surely insist he come, too, and the group would have what they wanted.

But staying here, staying put—would this night see her bedded? The queen wasn't alone in this body. Jayna was here. Jayna. Non-wife. A little hand-holding to facilitate the relationship was one thing, but lovemaking?

The king walked slowly toward her. She couldn't bring herself to look up. He stretched a hand down. She glanced at the long, brown fingers, the full forearm.

He caressed her cheek, then taking her arm, pulled her to her feet. She kept her head down, afraid to look into his eyes. Gently he pushed her hair away from her face. His hand moved softly along the curve of her neck, sending a rush of heat through her.

She met his gaze.

His lips claimed hers.

It was so easy. And the queen didn't fight her. The queen urged her on.

Why? Couldn't she do it on her own? Why did she have to work through *her*—making her feel these sensations, too? His mouth ravaged hers, his hands moving over her waist, her hips, her buttocks. His tongue thrust into her mouth, moist and wanton. Loving...

With a groan, she wrapped her arms around his neck and slid her hands down his back, searching his bare flesh with throbbing fingertips and aching palms. He filled her senses and took her senses...

His kiss robbed her of intellect, his tongue intimately plying the recesses of her mouth. His muscular body molded with her. Warm kisses lowered to her jaw, her chin.

Her breath halted in her throat as his hand glided over her breast, tightening her nipple within his palm. A hot trail of kisses moved over her neck and to the swell of her breast. His silky hair brushed sensually against her flesh as his mouth found her.

She pulled him close, her eyes closed, her body seeing all that needed seeing, feeling all that could be felt. She would become a woman tonight. And with no better a man. A cry escaped her before he reclaimed her lips with his and swept her into his arms. A moment later they were on the bed, the long, hard length of him pressed against her inner thigh. She would be wife in truth.

A scream rent the night.

Far beyond their window, but distinct nonetheless, a woman's scream sounded, again and again, each peal of distress more terrified than the last.

Amony leaped up. Adjusting his kilt, he headed for the bedroom door. Jayna followed. The pounding of running feet sounded outside the house. Amony flung open the front door and a guard stopped him short.

"What is it?"

"Farin went to check, Your Highness."

Amony turned to Jayna. "Stay here." He grasped her shoulders, his eyes bright. "Stay right here."

She nodded. He kissed her full on the lips, then turned to the guard. "Don't let her leave."

With that command, he stepped out into the darkness and disappeared around the corner of the house.

Maisha and Amony's attendant joined her in the doorway. "Is there anything we can do?"

Jayna glanced at Maisha. "Where's Penda?"

"Sound asleep."

Jayna looked back toward the darkness where Amony had gone. "I think we wait. The Pharaoh will be back in a moment."

But would he? Had Tiy and Rana devised their own method of luring Amony out into the night?

Jayna pressed a trembling hand to her mouth. They'd given her little time to do as they asked, but they didn't trust her, either. Were they so sure that one undenied kiss would make her no longer sympathetic to their cause?

Shouts sounded in the distance. Male voices. A moment later, Amony reappeared.

Relief rushed through Jayna.

"A lion is on the prowl," he told the guard, "so keep alert."

She stepped back into the house, her greedy gaze on Amony as he shut the door.

"Rana's servant, Deede, took a mauling." At the small group's collective gasp, he added, "She's fine. She wasn't bitten. Evidently, she had a rendezvous with someone in the men's quarters when the lion sprang. The villagers are launching a hunt. They don't let this sort of attack go ignored."

Jayna started to walk deeper into the house, but Amony didn't follow. She stopped and glanced back at him. "What are you doing?"

"Telling you good-bye."

"Good-bye?" His meaning sank in and alarm catapulted through her. "You're not going?"

He nodded.

Fear gripped her. Tiy and Rana wanted him outside, and Rana's servant was the woman mauled. Rana wouldn't set-up her own servant for possible death to draw Amony out, would she? No, it had to be an awful coincidence.

She watched with dismay as Amony's attendant presented him with his sandals.

"Are the nobles going?" she asked.

Amony looked up from fastening the lacings at his ankles. "All of them."

His attendant folded his hands and gave a bob of his head. "May I be of service, Your Highness?"

"There are hunters aplenty, Sone. You may seek your bed. It could be a long night."

The man nodded. "As you wish."

Jayna looked to Maisha. She needed time alone with Amony, time to beg him to stay. "You may retire, also, Maisha."

As soon as the servants were out of sight, she turned to Amony.

"Don't go!"

Rising, he pulled her into his arms. "Do you fear for me?"

"Yes," she said, her mouth dry, her palms sweaty against his thick shoulders. "You don't know how much I fear for you. Can I persuade you not to go?"

"Only the Pharaoh should stay at home and keep himself safe?"

"Yes."

He laughed.

"Did anyone see the lion?" she asked on a sudden thought.

"Deede, her gentleman friend, and a villager."

"A villager saw it?"

Amony nodded.

Jayna bowed her head, thinking. Maybe this attack was on the up-and-up. Maybe Amony would be all right with this other predator needing to be dealt with. Still, the thought of him wandering about in the presence of a savage lion did nothing to cheer her.

She looked up into his warm, dark eyes. "Your guard is going, of course?"

"Of course." His hand gently caressed her waist.

"I don't suppose women are allowed on this hunt?"

"Not this one."

"Don't do anything—" she struggled for words "—brave."

He laughed. "I'll look for the coward's way, at every moment."

"Don't tease me," she said, her heart pounding with dread. "Just be careful."

"I'll be careful." His gaze caressed her face. "As a matter of fact, I think I'll kill this lion myself. With my bare hands."

She knew what he meant. Desire still heated his eyes, and his hands moved over her, reminding her of the fire that still burned in her skin.

His head lowered, and she closed her eyes as his lips moved over hers in sweeping memory of their too brief moment in each other's arms. He released her slowly, then stepped away. At the door, he glanced back, his face tinged with regret. Then he was gone.

Jayna sat down on a chair.

The minutes ticked by to hours, and still she watched the door, wondering if the lion would take Amony, or if his unfaithful nobles would. This was the opportunity she'd intended to deny them. Anything could be done to Amony in the darkness.

I should have told him, she thought, over and over. *I should have told him.*

Visions of Amony bleeding, stumbling toward her, turned to visions of Daren and became jumbled. Her head pounded. Daren dead. Amony marked for death.

I should have told him, I should have told him.

Shortly before sunrise, loud, victorious voices filled the village. Jayna jumped up and rushed to the door. The guard smiled at her from the pre-dawn darkness.

"They're back."

"They got the lion?" she asked.

"They did."

She let the door close behind her and stepped away from the house. The villagers and their guests poured out of their mutual homes to watch the party return with the carcass of a large lion hung on a pole. Jayna's heart quickened as she searched the group for Amony's tall, muscular frame. There...in the middle...

Amony walked amongst them!

She fought the urge to run forward, an urge which nearly overwhelmed her with every passing second. How would the group respond to seeing her throw herself into Amony's arms? The man had gone off into the dark of night with his fiercest foes to fight a man-eating lion. If she was what she pretended to be, she should be sobbing in her hands at the incredible unfairness of his survival.

She could stand it no more. Turning, she ran back to the house and flung the door shut behind her. She dropped into the chair where she'd spent the night and buried her face in her hands.

He was alive!

The door opened.

She looked up.

Amony strode toward her, his face grim, his eyes questioning. "Jayna?" His voice was soft. "You ran when you saw me. Are you—angry?"

With the door closed against the cold, outside world, there was no reason to pretend. She ran to him and threw her arms around him. His strong arms closed around her waist. She squeezed her eyes shut at the delicious sensation.

"You're back," she whispered. "That's all I care about."

Amony drew his head back and touched a finger to her cheek. "What's this?"

She pulled out of his arms and wiped her eyes. She hadn't meant to cry.

"I'm so tired," she said. "I was so worried and tired. You must be tired."

She drew him toward the bedroom.

He was tired. She felt it in his slow gait, in the heaviness of his arm. She hugged him once more, and he smiled. He sat on the edge of the bed and she bent to remove his sandals.

"Come here." He pulled her away from the task. Stretching out on the bed, he lay on his side and drew her to him, cradling her tightly against his chest.

They were back where they started, and Amony was safe. Jayna's breath left her in a shaky sigh. She closed her scratchy, swollen eyes and couldn't bring them to re-open.

"Good-night," her king whispered softly.

Chapter Fifteen

They arrived at the palace mid-morning. The group had failed. Amony was alive. With light steps, and a lighter heart, Jayna walked to her chamber.

"Mamo!" As she expected, the man wandered near her door. He looked up at her in greeting.

She held out the mesh bag she carried. "I've brought you something." Stopping in front of him, she uncinched the neck of the bag.

"G'apes?" he asked.

"Yes. The most delicious grapes you'll ever taste," she said. "Try one."

He reached gingerly in.

"They're from Bene's estate upriver. He has the finest vineyard in the country. In the whole world, probably. I took one taste and thought of you. I had to bring you some." She laughed at the look of sheer pleasure that came over his face as he chewed the grape. "Perfect, isn't it?"

He nodded. "Mm-hmm."

She put the bag in his hands. "They're yours."

His head raised shyly. "Mine?"

She smiled and nodded.

Clutching the bag tighter, a broad smile spread over his face. "Mine." He backed away from her. "Mine."

She watched him walk away, then went into her chamber. Her priestesses met her through the connecting door.

"Welcome back, Your Highness."

"Did you have a nice trip?"

Jayna gasped at this last, recognizing the voice.

Orisa stood bright-eyed and smiling among the grinning women.

"You're back!" Jayna rushed forward to embrace her lady. Her *cousin*, she thought with affection as she squeezed her tight. She'd missed her. Until this moment, she hadn't realized how truly she valued this woman's presence in her life.

A half-hour later, the tales of their mutual trips related and discussed, Jayna let her ladies go about their own pursuits. Orisa remained behind. Jayna urged her toward a chair and took one next to her.

"Tell me how it went."

"Your mother is waiting," Orisa said. "She's staying at the little house outside Saqqara that Uncle uses during the flood. If you leave immediately—"

"Immediately?" Jayna asked, surprised.

Orisa nodded in understanding. "You just got back. This isn't too long a trip, though. If you leave soon, you could be there by afternoon and have the whole day to talk."

"And return in the morning," Jayna mused aloud.

Her cousin nodded. "You could be back by this time tomorrow, if you want."

Jayna thought about it. She hated the prospect of leaving Amony when they'd gotten so close, but the timing was perfect as far as his safety was concerned. The group needed to recover from their failure at killing him, and to develop a new plan. They would do nothing tonight, exhausted as they were from last night's bout with the lion. She was tired, too, but she had to do this. She needed to speak to the queen's mother and find out what she could about Daren's death.

She stood up. "I leave within the hour, then."

Orisa rose, too. "I was thinking." A shy look came over face. "It might be awkward explaining to your husband why you're going to your mother, rather than she coming here. Had you thought of it?" At Jayna's hesitation, Orisa's face lit up. "I have. We used to play there when we were young. It was so much fun, don't you think?"

Jayna smiled, certain that it had been. "Of course."

To her relief, her cousin didn't press to share remembrances, but continued on her original course. "I was thinking that you could tell Amony you have a longing to see the old playhouse again. I could go with you, if you wish, to make it look proper."

"I shouldn't tell him I'm visiting Mother?"

Orisa's mouth dropped open. "You want to tell him?"

Jayna shook her head, though she wondered why she shouldn't want to tell him. Did Amony know how her mother felt about him? "I'll use your plan," she said. "I'd love to have you with me."

***

Standing inside the reception room door, Jayna was acutely and uncomfortably aware that she had intruded upon a meeting of province leaders. There was no help for it. She had to leave, and she couldn't go without saying good-bye.

At last, Amony handed the papyrus he held to the man next to him and excused himself. Jayna watched him rise, worried he'd be upset at the interruption, but his eyes met hers, and he smiled.

"My Queen." He stopped before her, his gaze warm.

She wasted no time. "I need to go away."

His smile faded. "Where do you need to go?"

"Away with my lady, Orisa."

"Your cousin?"

"Yes. Just until tomorrow." She gave the story Orisa had supplied. "Uncle's little house is open and the two of us—we wish to see it again. It's been a long time since we played there as children. I wish to revisit it."

His brow raised. "Your childhood?"

His meaning sank in, and she smiled. "No. Just the place."

He remained silent a moment, then took her arm and led her aside, farther out of hearing distance of the group at the table. "Are you running from me, Jayna?"

"No," she said quickly, then lowered her voice. "If I was running, it wouldn't be away from you."

"Then why go? Why now?" He started to reach for her shoulders, then hesitated. Frustration twisted his face as he lowered his hands and whispered, "Can't this journey wait a while?"

She knew what he meant, how he was feeling. They were just making headway in their relationship, and she was going away. "I'm sorry," she said. "It's important that I go now."

He shook his head. "I don't understand."

And she couldn't explain. "I'm sorry," she said again.

He sighed. Lifting his hand, and heedless of who might see, he slid his fingers up her arm.

Her skin tingled from his touch.

Catching the ends of her hair, he wrapped a lock around his index finger. "I can't deny you."

She met his warm gaze. "Thank you."

"Come back to me."

Her heart ached at the plea. She had nowhere else she wanted to be, but for the moment, she couldn't tell him that. She had to speak to the queen's mother.

She nodded. "I'll be back."

Amony released her hair. His warm palm cupped her shoulder, then slid down her arm to her hand. Gathering her fingers, he lifted them.

Resentful of the others in the room, Jayna swallowed heavily as his lips touched her palm.

His eyes burned with desire as he released her.

"Good day, Your Highness," she whispered as she backed away from him.

***

Though the smallest of the royal vessels, the craft was worthy of the short jaunt down the Nile. Orisa sat beside Jayna on a broad, cushioned lounge. Two guardsmen sat before them and behind them. The girls ignored them as they talked and snacked on cucumber slices. Two hours past noon they reached the outskirts of Saqqara. They docked and took an overland route ten minutes due west until they reached a large, whitewashed mansion hugged tight by vine-draped sycamores.

Having just left the place, Orisa took the lead and drew her cousin up the path to the front door. As she awaited the answering of the knock on the door, Jayna felt suddenly nervous. The mother was there, beyond the stout wood.

The door swung open, and Jayna stared into the face she'd hunted for in the mirror that first day in the queen's chamber. Her own face. Fuller lips, pointed chin. Brown eyes.

"Mother," the word left her in a rush.

"My daughter!"

Arms wrapped around Jayna in a hug so fierce and full of longing that it brought tears to her eyes. She hugged the woman back and breathed in her fragrance.

Mother...tagging along at her skirt while she spoke with the servants...sitting on a tall stool while watching a woman apply kohl to her mother's eyes and rogue to her cheeks.

The queen's heart pulsed and twisted inside her at the vivid memories.

Or was it her own heart?

Eerie, fantastic feelings swept through Jayna. Impossible, incredible thoughts. The authorities had never been able to locate the woman who'd left her an orphan on the steps at Boston U. Her abandonment had been in all the papers, but no one had ever responded. In that crowded area, that popular place, no one had seen anything, or anyone. Was this why?

Because her mother was here, four thousand years in the past?

With a depth of emotion she hadn't even imagined, she felt her love for this woman. Mother. Her mother? Her birth mother?

No. She rejected the idea swiftly. She only felt the *queen's* feelings. What she considered wasn't possible. A child born in the twentieth century could lay no claim to a mother who lived in this age.

And how is it possible that you're here this very minute?

The intrusive thought nagged her as she looked at the woman. "I'm so glad to see you, Mother."

"Oh, Jayna." Tears welled from eyes slightly lined with age. "I've missed you so. Come in. Our meal is all prepared."

* * *

"How is Father?" Jayna asked, poking at the last of her grilled beef.

The older woman set her goblet next to her plate and sighed. "He's come to terms with Daren's death." She nodded, thoughtful as she gazed past Jayna to the open window. "He's getting better. Almost back to normal. But he doesn't know about your marriage. He thinks you're away, staying with friends. I'm afraid what telling him the truth would bring."

"What is the truth, Mother?"

Orisa stiffened in her chair and carefully laid down her napkin. Jayna took warning from her cousin's reaction.

Her mother's dark gaze returned to her and grew sad. "The truth is, you've sacrificed your life to bring low your brother's killer." Her eyelids dipped, then rose. "I know, Jayna. I didn't understand at first. I accused you of terrible things, but I was wrong. I know what you intend, though how you intend it, I can't imagine." She shook her head. "I'm sorry. You didn't deserve the things I said to you. I'll never forgive myself."

"How will you feel if I do as you think I intend?"

"I'm frightened for you. I would rather you give up this path than pursue it. I don't want to lose both of my children to that evil man."

Jayna folded her hands in her lap. "It must be difficult for you to keep such slurs to yourself. No countryman could like hearing such words."

The brown eyes shadowed with doubt, and the gentle voice took on a tense undercurrent. "Have you taken offense, Daughter?"

"I think of your safety, Mother."

"Don't worry for me. I don't have to live with him. But I wonder. Are you taking steps that will leave you blameless?"

Angry, Jayna pushed away from the table. "I won't discuss this." She rose and glanced at her cousin. "Close your ears, Orisa."

"Perhaps I should leave." Her cousin rose from the table and hurried from the room.

"Why are you so upset?" the elder woman asked. "You need to know that your father and I will be ready for you when you need us. We know many people. We can flee this Pharaoh's anger. He hurt us; he's taken one of us; but it doesn't have to continue. Orisa knows how to contact me. You can come to us at anytime. If need be, we'll find other shores. He won't hurt you, if only you'll come to us."

Jayna turned away. Her mother—yes, in this role of queen, the woman was her mother—did believe she intended to see Amony dead.

Keeping her back turned, she asked, "What do you know of Daren's life just before his death? Had he expressed any opinion on Amony at all?"

"He didn't know to hate him, as we do."

Jayna looked down at the potted plant before her on the window ledge, but didn't see its lush, green leaves and delicate blue flowers for the encouraging vision of a brother with no animosity for her husband. "What did he know?" she asked.

"He knew how to be vizier. He should have been vizier."

"Instead of Yera?"

"Yera!" The name issued forth with such venom that Jayna turned to view her mother. "With Hasson as rightful king, Yera would be scrounging in the desert rocks with his scorpion friends."

Jayna shook her head. What had she missed? "Hasson as king?" she asked.

"A general among generals." The dark gaze moved past her again. "The people had no idea what they were doing when they chose Amony instead. He only fooled them. We know how little a Pharaoh he truly is."

"Why would he kill Daren, Mother?"

"To be king."

"But—" Jayna halted, confused. "Daren didn't want to be king. Did he?"

"Hasson!" Her mother's gaze focused on her as she said sharply, "Hasson would be king."

"What has this to do with Daren?"

The dark eyes hardened with suspicion. "You've fallen for his tricks, after all, haven't you? You—"

"Mother!" Jayna put up her hands to ward off the verbal onslaught. "I'm just—" she took a deep breath and lowered her voice. "I'm just confused."

The elder relaxed back in her chair, but eyed her with a bitterness Jayna hoped wasn't aimed at her. "Hasson fought as bravely as any general to free us from those pale devils. Amony killed Hasson and Daren that the people's hearts would turn to him."

Jayna moistened her lips, almost afraid to speak. "Why Daren?"

Her mother thumped a hand on the tabletop. "A Pharaoh is his vizier, as much as a vizier is his Pharaoh. Have you lived so long and not known this?"

Jayna knew it. She knew it from every history book she'd touched in years, from every pyramid she'd ever entered. And, still, her mother had to pound it into her head.

But what did it mean? Yera was Amony's vizier, and Yera sought Amony's death.

Would Yera, right hand to Amony, become king if Amony died? The history books provided no answer to this shadowy period on the Egyptian timeline.

It made sense, though.

Jayna turned away again, thinking.

With Amony dead, Yera would be the most powerful man in Egypt, if only temporarily. What had the rest of the group to gain in conspiring with him? A viziership for one of them if Yera became king? Favors for the others that perhaps Amony wouldn't grant?

Jayna nodded with the force of her convictions. Amony was innocent.

A smile stole over her, and she gently brushed the dust from the rich green leaves of a potted plant with the most beautiful and delicate blue flowers she'd ever seen.

Amony hadn't killed her brother nor ordered his slaying. He was innocent.

But she'd known that.

She knew it.

And she'd prove it.

She turned and looked at her mother. A faraway look haunted the woman's dark eyes.

Thinking of Orisa's warnings, and her own glimpse of the strong reaction her mother had to any pro-Amony comment, she hesitated.

She couldn't tell her mother the truth yet. Not until she could get her proof.

Chapter Sixteen

She was twenty-one years old and she'd had several boyfriends, but none of them were right for her. She'd laughed with them, played golf or tennis or bowled with them, but she'd never fallen in love with any of them. The boys had asked her out. Then as she got older, the men had asked her out, and to bed. She never went. It was never right.

Until he came.

No! He hadn't come to *her*. The dream wasn't hers!

Lying in the plump bed, Jayna awakened at the strength of her reaction. But fighting to keep her eyes open proved fruitless. She was tired...so tired...and she really did want to see what the woman inside her had to show...

She hadn't expected to like him, much less love him. The loving came later. The like was immediate. She'd resented it. He was handsome, more handsome than any man she'd ever seen, but that had only a bit to do with it. She knew handsome. Handsome was cocksure and inflated. Handsome was thinking everything one saw in a looking glass was all that was needed. Handsome equaled ugliness. Better she should fall for an ugly man who cared for his insides.

He wasn't that way, though. He'd met her with the greatest humility, his handsome features seeming to mean nothing to him, as if he had no awareness of his beauty. He was kind. And he watched her, looking at her with eyes that told her she was the most beautiful, graceful woman in the world. Though he had to have been bold, he was...

What was he?

He was almost shy with her. He was gentle, certainly. She'd expected ego and a loud voice. He'd been a man of character and depth. A man of honor. A man she could love.

But he hadn't come. Not to her!

She'd fooled him. Or had she fooled herself? Warm kisses on cool nights, cool kisses in the heat of day, wouldn't turn her from her task. She wouldn't be fooled. Not she.

'Jayna.'

'I thought you'd never come.'

'I've waited forever.'

The voices woke her.

She sat up and looked around in confusion. She was in her uncle's house. In bed. Alone. Releasing her breath, she brushed her hair out of her face. Sweat dampened the linen beneath her. Her sheets entangled her thighs.

Freeing her feet, she stood and got out of bed. She needed air. She needed to cool off.

Stepping out the back door of the house, she glanced around. The snorts and croaks of wildlife discouraged her from venturing out onto the grounds, but the porch seemed safe enough.

I've waited forever. The words from her dream came back to haunt her.

"Jayna."

She halted mid-stride along the porch. His voice. Amony.

She blinked. He was there, really there, standing ten feet away from her on the lawn, a pleated, white kilt and a pair of sandals his only adornment. Her husband. Her lover. The man who invaded her thoughts and dreams.

"What—" She shook her head, unable to believe her eyes. "What are you doing here?"

No mirage, was her husband. No dream. Flesh-and-blood potent masculinity bounded up the stairsteps.

Strong hands grasped her shoulders. "Where is he?"

Dazed, she asked, "Why did you come?"

"I waited too long," he breathed. Then angrily, his fingers pressing deeper around her shoulders, he said, "I've waited forever."

I've waited forever. Jayna stared at him in surprise. "What do you mean *forever*?"

A hard gleam entered his eyes, and his lean cheeks tightened. "Just tell me where he is."

Confusion clouded Jayna's brain. "Where who is?"

"Nassor."

"Nassor?" she repeated, stunned. "Why would I know where Nassor is?"

His hands fell away from her. The storm that ravaged his face softened as he witnessed her surprise. "He's not here?"

"Why would he be here?"

"He left only hours after you did."

"Not to come here."

Amony looked away, but not before she caught the flash of relief in his eyes. His gaze returned to her, his expression penitent. "I'm sorry."

"You thought I was meeting him?"

After a long pause, he nodded.

Jayna couldn't help smiling. Amony was jealous at the thought she might be seeing another man.

"My King," she said, "how could you think it?"

The Pharaoh had difficulty meeting her gaze. "The coincidence." He shrugged awkwardly. "The obviousness."

She laughed. "Oh goodness! What would you have done if you'd found him here?"

"I'd have killed him." Amony met her gaze boldly, a hint of his torment blazing from his eyes. Her smile faded as his gaze fell away. "I would have tried to restrain myself from killing him," he said. "Then I would have banished him to some far corner of the earth where you could never find him."

His words filled her with tenderness. And pride. He wouldn't have killed the man, but he would have done everything else in his power to keep her faithful to him.

She reached out, feeling her heart race as she did, and pressed her palm to his sturdy chest. "I have no interest in Nassor."

His eyes flashed, and he closed his hand over hers. Delicious warmth flooded through her. Gently, he stroked the back of her hand. "Who does interest you?"

His fingers moved down her wrist, his palm cupping the flesh of her forearm, sending shivers of delight through her.

"Would you be surprised to hear I've set my sights on the Pharaoh?"

He drew her into the circle of his strong arms. His gaze moved over her eyes, then fell to her lips. "I'd be honored, Your Highness."

His head neared ever-so-slowly. His gaze raised to meet hers, and she watched him until their lips touched. Closing her eyes, she gave herself to the sensation of his moist mouth claiming hers, his hands pressing her against his firm body. She molded into him, her arms around his neck. With her fingertips, she sought the silky hair at his nape. His strong neck shifted beneath her hands, his head moving.

Warm moisture met her neck, sensual lips plying her flesh, and she arched against the wild pleasure of it. His hair brushed her jaw, and she moved her head into the sensation, running her cheek against the black silk until his lips claimed hers again. His tongue slipped inside her mouth, jolting, delicious, turning, tasting, then left her for a storm of small kisses at the corner of her mouth.

The promises of the past night begged to be filled.

"Where are your guards?" she asked.

"I came alone," he returned huskily.

"What?" She pulled her head back to look at him.

His clouded gaze moved from her lips to her eyes. "I had a boatman, but I left my guard at the palace."

Alarm tingled through Jayna. "You didn't even bring one?"

"No."

The thought of the harm any of the group could have perpetrated on him chilled her. Little planning would be necessary to do away with a man with no witnesses. He had to have slipped out of the palace without a word to anyone who meant him harm, and without being seen. She stepped out of his embrace and rubbed the bumps that rose on her arms. "That was dangerous."

He pulled her back to him and warmed her arms himself. "I'm fine."

She rested her hands on his sturdy, sculpted chest. He was fine. She couldn't imagine anything happening to this strong, virile man.

The memory of a sarcophagus gleaming in a dark tomb returned to her, the reality hitting her like a fist in the belly. A moan escaped her as she dropped her forehead against his chest.

"What is it?" Worry edged Amony's voice as he tightened his arms around her.

She had to tell him.

She looked into his eyes. Was it love that shone back at her? Was it love she felt twisting so painfully, and so exquisitely, inside her? How could she shatter this? How could she do or say anything to lose a moment of this beautiful feeling between them?

He'd made it here safely. He was in no danger. She could remain quiet a little while longer. If only for this night, her secret would stay with her.

"What's wrong?" he prodded gently.

She shook her head. "Nothing. I just worry for you."

A scream shattered the air. *Again?* Jayna could only believe the word that ran through her mind went also through Amony's.

Her mother stood in the doorway, her finger pointed at the Pharaoh. "Get out of here! Get away from my daughter. Get away from this house!"

"Mother, this is Amony!" Jayna reprimanded harshly. "You're speaking to the King of Egypt. Collect yourself!"

Amony stretched forth a hand. "Madam. I'm sorry—"

Lurching back from his touch, her mother turned and fled inside. Jayna glanced at Amony. "Just a moment." She hurried inside after her mother and caught her arm. "What was that?"

"I want him gone!" the woman panted. "Now."

"He's my husband," Jayna said. "Would you arouse his suspicion by treating him so?"

"I don't care what he does to me."

Jayna tried blackmail. "What about me?"

Her mother pulled out of her grasp. "I won't have him here. I want him gone."

Jayna gaped at her mother. The woman's hate ran deep, indeed. "The Pharaoh isn't going anywhere tonight," she said. "It's dark, and he's alone. We'll leave at first light."

"You're so concerned for his well-being?" It was her mother's turn to look shocked. When Jayna didn't deny the charge, her mother's face hardened. "He's gotten to you, as I said. Hasn't he?" A scowl twisted her mouth. "You're not your brother's sister."

Pain jolted through Jayna. "You're being cruel, Mother."

Orisa stepped into the room, her eyes puffy with sleep. She glanced at the two glaring women. "Have I intruded, or may I help?"

"Yes," Jayna said. She took her cousin's arm. "Amony is out on the porch—alone! Go to him. Keep an eye on him." The dominant thought in her mind was his safety. If anyone had managed to follow him....

Orisa stepped out the doorway, and Jayna turned to her mother. After several minutes, she'd calmed the woman and made her see the ridiculousness of trying to send Amony away.

"I'll not have the two of you bedding down under the same roof as I," her mother capitulated. "You won't dishonor me so."

"I had no such intentions," Jayna said and wondered if she lied.

"Bring him in, then. A servant will show him to a room other than yours, else I'll burn this villa to the ground."

Jayna let out a deep sigh. Daren's killer had seriously damaged her family.

She heeded her mother's warning, seeing Amony set up in a room across from hers with a servant to guard his door. Far away from court intrigues, she wasn't going to still fear for Amony's life at her mother's hand.

She told Amony her mother sometimes had attacks of hysteria that had nothing to do with reality, but that not seeing him would soothe her. Her affliction was man-based, and Amony was, she explained with much discomfort, very much a man. She left him believing she was staying in her mother's chamber to comfort her.

***

They left at dawn as Jayna had promised. Her mother stayed in her private chamber, so as not to encounter the man she hated. She and Amony didn't speak of the night past. Orisa's presence precluded any intimate discussion, but something had changed between King and Queen. Their relationship since the trip to the Delta had grown more intimate. The physical manifestation of that was also growing. Jayna had to believe it was only a matter of time before she—no, the queen—was a wife in full.

In the quiet moments of the return trip she felt Amony's gaze on her and knew what he was thinking. Her thoughts weren't far away.

Chapter Seventeen

That afternoon, a servant came by and asked Jayna to accompany him to the Pharaoh's chamber for the midday meal. Sending her priestesses to the dining room, she followed the man. As the servant pushed the door open, Yera brushed rudely past in his haste to quit the room. A scowl drew his thin brows together as he clutched a disorderly pile of papyrus to his chest.

Jayna rubbed her arm where his skin had touched hers, and a frown wrinkled her brow when she stepped into the reception room. Amony looked up from where he stood at the table. His mood seemed no better than Yera's, but seeing her, his face softened and he smiled.

"You came."

"You didn't think I would?"

"I hoped you would." He took her hands in his. He gazed into her eyes a moment, then pressed a kiss to the back of her hand. "I haven't much time. I've been gone so much these past few days. But I thought we could take our meal together."

"I'd like that."

Amony nodded at his steward. Within seconds, servants had a hearty meal laid out on the table. Amony led her forward and pulled back her chair. She sat lightly in it, and he pushed it forward before taking a seat across from her.

She ate a little, then asked what most absorbed her. "Did all not go well with your vizier?"

Amony eyed her quizzically.

She shrugged. "He looked upset when we passed at the door." Watching Amony closely, she didn't miss the sobering of his features.

He shook his head. "It's nothing. We had a—difference of opinion—you might say. That's all."

"That's all?" she asked.

He nodded and took a drink from his goblet.

"What was the opinion?"

Amony returned the vessel to the table and sighed. "What wasn't? It seems we differ over everything these days."

"Why?" She felt as if she was pressing the matter, but as long as he was willing to discuss Yera, she'd ask. "Has something happened between the two of you?"

Amony stared at her a long moment, his eyes troubled. "I speak in the strictest confidence."

She leaned forward. A confidence? Something he would share with his wife that he shared with no one else? Her heart swelled with pride. He trusted her!

"What is it?" she asked gently. "Your words will go no farther than this room."

"I wouldn't have chosen Yera as vizier. Did you know that?"

He watched her closely, and Jayna frowned. She shook her head.

His gaze dropped, and the corners of his mouth twisted downward. "He was pushed upon me. Popular opinion. The province leaders. Everyone assumed he would be vizier because he served beside me."

"In the war," she added what she knew.

He nodded. "He is suited to the position. He has a way with people and an organized mind. It's just—"

He appeared to want to say no more.

"What?" she asked. "What is it?"

"I often think he operates outside the law." He shrugged. "I've never seen anything, but he navigates so close, I have to wonder."

"What has he done?"

Amony sighed. "He comes to me with requests of land and valuables for councilmen who've done nothing more extraordinary than any other councilman. Negotiations with the Nubians were nearing an end, yet I found out, just now, that while I was gone, a troop of our soldiers wandered across the border. The reasoning for it was shaky at best. Yera supported the resulting bloodshed." He shook his head. "His reaction was a far cry from our efforts at the table."

"You think he had a hand in it?"

"I've been suspicious of his motivations in many matters, lately."

Jayna drew in a deep breath. He suspected Yera of wrongdoing, just as she did. He'd believe her. She could tell him what he'd done to Daren—what he planned for *him*!

A knock sounded at the door, then the steward peered in. "Your Highness, your guests are here."

Jayna looked to Amony. "Guests?"

"My next meeting," he said. "A group of ranchers from the Delta." He looked to his steward. "Where are they?"

"In the main hall."

"Have them taken to the council room. I'll be along in a moment."

The servant disappeared. Jayna rose. Amony moved to her side and pulled her chair back. She smiled up at him, acutely aware of his long, lean form so close to her.

He slipped his arms around her. "Thank you for coming. I fear I won't see you the rest of the day."

"You'll be so busy?" she asked.

"I've played too much." His gaze moved to her lips. "And too little."

"Perhaps—later?" Her heart fluttered at her boldness.

His gaze raised to hers, open and questioning. When his mouth swept down on hers, she suspected he saw what she wanted him to see.

***

The kiss stayed with her. All afternoon, the taste of his lips and the feel of his mouth moving across hers, inflamed her senses. She had duties of her own to attend to, but she went about them distracted. At last, with the day done, she was left to herself. The Pharaoh, she'd been informed, was still in his council room, settling some matter between two wealthy merchants from Hermopolis.

Wandering through the flower garden outside the east wing of the palace, she came upon a plant that surprised her. Four plump red tomatoes ripened on a vine in the early evening twilight. *Tomatoes in a flower garden?* she puzzled. Plucking the largest of the fruit, she tore it open and smelled it. Tomato, as she knew it. She took a bite and smiled at the tangy flavor. No such delicacy ever graced the royal tables. Had the tomato not yet been discovered for its edible qualities?

Taking another bite, the heady taste of a stuffed-crust, Mama Cleo's pizza with extra sauce filtered through her mind and left her mouth watering. Could she...? What sort of ingredients were available? Enough, she decided, and plucked two more of the tomatoes. Hurrying back inside, she located the kitchen.

A sturdy woman, broad of hip and leg, stopped her in the doorway. "Your Highness, I'm the kitchen guardian. May I help you?"

Jayna explained her desire to create a special dish, and the woman grudgingly allowed her entrance. Lighting an additional lamp to drive back the shadows, she stared at the tomatoes in Jayna's hands.

"What are you doing with those?"

Though it took some heavy talking, Jayna convinced the woman the fruit wasn't poisonous. Fifteen minutes later, she was deep in flatbread, goatcheese, and finely diced beef. Her greatest challenge lay in the creation of the tomato sauce, and she rejected one spice after another in search of just the right flavoring. Marijani, as the woman had introduced herself, finally gave up on her and, laughing, turned the kitchen over to her while she went to relieve herself.

Jayna smiled as the woman waved at the door. Meeting Marijani had been like coming face-to-face with an army drill sergeant, a far cry from the lady who held her sides until she needed to pee—and quickly.

Yet, left alone, Jayna's thoughts turned serious.

Two issues, sorely neglected this entire day, begged attention. First was her belief that she could finally warn Amony. He distrusted Yera and trusted her. She could tell him. Somehow. Carefully, to be sure. She'd tell him what she suspected about Yera. She could say he'd come to her while their marriage was so distant and tried to gain her support. And she had to name all the conspirators, but just how without incriminating herself, proved a difficult puzzle. Atop that, she had to come up with a worthy explanation for why she hadn't brought the knowledge to him sooner.

The second issue—here, too, she faltered. The second issue was the desire for Amony that had grown to overwhelming proportions within her. Though the word 'adultery' came to mind, it wouldn't hold. The queen's need drove her, dominated her, consumed her. Jayna didn't understand it, but she knew it. The queen wanted—needed—to make love to her husband before he heard of the plot on his life. Jayna had brought them together, and she would bring them closer still. All of them.

Her thoughts fixated on the man. She had a mission. She had to tell him what he needed to know. But she and the queen—she, the queen—would make love to Amony.

Jayna's hands trembled. She swallowed heavily, then glanced up at a sound from the door Marijana had gone through.

"Oh, there you are," Orisa said, surprised.

Jayna pressed her hands together to still their shaking. "Did you need something?"

"The new cloth came in while you were gone. The dressmaker sent me to find out which you wanted for your robe."

Jayna looked at the swatches bunched in her cousin's hand. "Bring them here."

"Step into Marijani's kitchen without permission?" The dark eyes rounded. "I don't think I will. Only Her Highness could get near."

Jayna laughed. "Fine. I'll come to you." Dusting her hands, she followed her cousin through the archway. A small table rested on the inside wall. Orisa laid out the fabrics. "Which one for your robe?"

"The gold one," Jayna said, then bit her lip.

"What?" Orisa noticed her action. "Not the gold?"

Amony's bed was done in gold, the vision of such making her decision. Why did her heart flutter with fear alongside her excitement?

"The gold," she repeated, halting further thought on that matter.

Parting from her cousin, she went back to the kitchen. The sauce for her pizza wasn't quite right. She tried a sample from another jar, then another, until the taste neared what she wanted. Applying the layers: flatbread, sauce, cheese, beef, she then stuck the pan wherein it rested above the fire in the hearth and set about cleaning up.

Marijani returned. "You're done."

"Yes." Jayna picked up the last few amphorae of spices from the table and returned them to their shelves. Marijani helped her wash up the table, and before long, the pizza was done.

"Would you like a taste?" Jayna asked.

The woman looked at her, wary.

"I promise it won't hurt you. Watch this." She picked up a slice and took a bite. "Mmm." The combined flavors were as satisfying as she'd anticipated. Pleased with herself, she nodded at Marijani. "It's really good."

The woman took a slice of her own. Chewing slowly, she finally exclaimed, "It is good! I've never tasted anything like it. You'll have to give this recipe to the cooks."

"Do you want some more?"

Marijani put up her hand. "No. I supped late as it is. This is all for me."

Jayna looked at her half-eaten slice, then back to the woman. "Do you think the Pharaoh would like it?"

"How could he not?"

"Maybe I should take him some." Jayna kept her gaze averted. "In his chamber."

"A good idea," Marijani said. "Cook said he hadn't stopped to dine tonight."

Jayna's head shot up. "He didn't?"

"Not from what I heard."

Standing up, Jayna self-consciously smoothed her gown.

"You look fine, Your Highness."

Marijani's eyes glowed with understanding.

Jayna smiled. "I suppose I should take him a drink to go with it."

Together they fetched a goblet of wine. Marijani handed her the platter they'd put the pizza on. Jayna took a deep breath.

"It's delicious," the woman said. "He'll be very pleased."

Jayna smiled. "Thank you. For everything."

Marijani waved away her thanks.

Jayna crossed the kitchen, pizza and wine glass in hand, and made her way through the dining room. A right, then another, and she'd be at Amony's chamber. Did she look presentable, or had Marijani been kind? Should she go to her chamber first?

And chicken out, letting this night pass her by entirely?

She made the right turn, instead of the left that would lead her to her chamber. She only wanted to take him a snack. A light repast. If she kept that in mind, she'd make it.

"Food," she told the guard at his door. "I've brought the Pharaoh a small repast."

He pushed the door open for her. Amony wasn't in his reception room. "I've brought the Pharaoh a small repast," she repeated for the inner guard.

He stepped around and guided the door open.

Oil lamps drove the darkness from the room and bathed it in a gentle orange glow. Amony turned, his hand sweeping his headdress to the table near his bed. He had the look of having just entered the chamber himself. The weary expression on his face transformed, his eyes lighting up beneath a surprised smile.

"Jayna."

"I brought you something to eat," she said. "I made it myself. It's a—an old family recipe."

"Thank you." His smooth voice pulled at her heartstrings. "You can set it anywhere."

Jayna passed by the table and chairs, growing steadily insecure. What was he thinking to see her walk past the obvious choice? She kept going, all the way to the back of his room.

"How about here?" She sat down on his bed, placed the wine on the side table, and looked over at him.

His wary eyes watched her.

He moved forward slowly, as if too fast an approach would send her fleeing. Carefully, he eased near her and, just as carefully, lowered himself to the mattress.

She smiled and felt her lips tremble. Pursing them together, she raised the pizza toward him. "Won't you try it?"

He looked it over. "You had some already?"

She nodded. "I'm not very hungry, though. I thought maybe you'd be hungry."

His eyes didn't leave her. "I'm hungry."

She swallowed and looked down at the pizza. Lowering it to her lap, she pulled a slice free and handed it to him. His palm lingered under her hand. She pulled away slowly.

His gaze dipped, then he took a bite. His gaze flickered. "Mmm, this is good."

She smiled. "I hoped you'd like it."

She watched him a moment, then gazed around the chamber. A lump lodged in her throat and her knees shook.

Amony folded the remainder of the thin slice of crust, reducing it to a single bite.

"Would you like some more?" She thrust the pizza toward him. His dark gaze rested so intently on her that she lowered the pizza back to her lap.

"Thank you." Surprising her, his tan arm crossed in front of her. She felt the pressure from his lean fingers through the plate, making it rest subtly heavier on her thighs. His face hovered nearer as he leaned to take the slice, his gaze searching hers. She drew a deep breath as he pulled back.

He chewed and watched her. Tension wrapped around her. He took a bite, inadvertently leaving a dab of sauce on his mouth. She reached out to wipe it away, and a sudden, deep tugging in her chest made her hand linger. She wiped the spot away slowly, and his gaze turned serious, heated. She pulled her hand away. Bright sauce covered her finger. She put it in her mouth.

Amony's gaze darkened. As though mesmerized, he placed his slice of pizza back on the plate, then lifted the plate from her lap. His arm continued on past her, his thigh pressing against hers, as he slid the tray to the table near the bed. He drew back with the wine goblet in his long fingers.

Jayna watched his profile as he drank, her gaze drawn to the rich gleam of his hair in the light of the oil lamps. He lowered the vessel, then stretched across her again to return it to the table.

This time he didn't lean back.

Red-brown eyes looked into hers.

She couldn't breathe for the promise she saw there.

"Jayna," he whispered. His gaze moved over her face, tenderly, passionately. Then his lips captured hers, and he pressed her back upon the cushions.

Ecstasy swept through Jayna's soul as she returned her husband's passion, her breath escaping her in a moan as his kiss moved to her jawline, her throat. The thick sinew of his back shifted under her questing hand as he claimed her body with his, with his lips and his hands. Broad shoulders flexed beneath her fingers, beneath her lips, as she pulled him to her, intent on exploring him as thoroughly as he explored her.

Their mouths met hungrily and with greed.

Desire, the need for one another *and no other*, shook them to their foundations, to the center of their souls and back again, as flesh met flesh. Heart met heart.

The outer-world ceased to exist.

Panted breaths mingled, bodies molded, then joined. Straining, reaching.

That which was sought was found, that yearned for, claimed. Love, in yet another of its many wondrous forms, was blissfully, breathlessly made between the king and Jayna—his queen.

Chapter Eighteen

She awakened slowly to the dark room, a hot glow of contentment inside her. Moving against the sheets, she remembered the feel of her lover's skin against hers. Stretching a hand toward Amony, she encountered his muscular torso, and passion swirled anew within her. They'd made love for most of the night. Morning would come soon.

She had to tell him the truth in the morning.

Staring through the darkness, she envisioned a reversal of roles. Amony, the man she single-mindedly loved, confessed to conspiring to kill *her*. Despite the passion still warming her skin and firing her mind, his declarations of love would mean little.

Panic slammed through her.

Did she really expect words of love to outweigh such horrible intentions? Even if she kept silent about her involvement, he would find out about her through the others. Surely they wouldn't let her walk away from this unscathed.

Stiffling a moan, she threw back the silk sheet.

After the night she and Amony had just shared—the love, the passion! Oh, virgin that she'd been, she'd had no idea what she was letting herself in for.

Lovemaking was a double-edged sword. It could join two souls, and it could separate them forever. How could this confession of hers do anything less?

She pressed her hands against her forehead and stared down at Amony's still form. What a fool she'd been! She and the queen!

She had to go. She had to re-think this! Catching up her gown, she headed for the door, pulling it on as she went. She ignored the guards and rushed out into the corridor.

Back in her own chamber, she leaned breathless against her inner door.

Why, why, why did this have to be between them?

Pushing upright, she paced the length of her room and back again.

She'd gone to him, knowing her night in his arms could be her first and her last. All that mattered, truly, was that he lived. Maybe she could no longer be his queen. Maybe he'd uncover the truth of her part in the conspiracy and turn on her, sentencing her to the very death she'd sought for him.

So be it.

But she would have her say.

She'd confess her love.

She looked around at her chamber. There was nothing but emptiness, an emptiness she'd felt since the day she walked in here almost a year before. A bride stepping into her lonely chambers, chambers she'd insisted be apart from her husband's. She'd done that. She. Jayna. The Queen. And she'd been wrong about it. She'd been wrong about a lot of things.

Jayna smiled, then laughed at the memory that held no distance from her. Joy bubbled up inside her. And amazement.

I belong here, don't I? This is my life. I got sidetracked into the future, but somehow it's helped. I love him. I've always loved him.

"The queen and I are one," she said, knowing the truth at last, and with all her heart.

Two memories, two lifetimes, one woman.

"I've been sent back to my previous life and given a second chance."

She drew a deep breath.

"I won't let him die this time. I won't!"

Chapter Nineteen

Dawn streaked the sky outside her windows when she returned down the corridor. Strangely, two guards rather than one, now stood duty outside the door. Atep rushed out of the room.

"There she is. Come!" He waved her forward. "Come quickly."

His urgency alarmed her. She ran to meet him.

"The Pharaoh's alive," he said, "but he's been poisoned."

Jayna's legs gave way beneath her. The guard caught her, and she fought to straighten. Her head spun, and the faces before her blurred.

"No," she panted. "No—"

Atep shook her shoulders. "He's alive, do you hear me?"

"He's—alive," Jayna repeated, forcing herself to believe him, forcing herself to believe that it wasn't too late. She grasped the healer's arm. "Let me see him."

Atep pulled her into the chamber she'd left only a couple of hours before. Three men hovered about the bed—none from the group. She shoved her way to the bedside. Amony lay very still and very pale.

"Oh god." The dizziness hit her again.

Atep swung her around. She fought waves of gray that threatened to take her consciousness.

"Either the dose wasn't lethal, or he didn't consume enough. What did he eat last night? The guard claimed you brought him food."

Jayna blinked. He was asking about the pizza. She looked at the plate with the single slice remaining. In her husband's arms she'd wanted for nothing, but he had missed his dinner, and his stomach growled so loudly that he'd had to eat more. Half-sitting, reclined against the stack of pillows, he'd held her tightly to his side and eaten all but that one slice. Tears blurred her eyes.

Following her gaze, Atep stepped over to the table and picked up the platter. "Did you eat any of this?"

She nodded. "A little."

"You have no symptoms?"

"No."

"We'll have to round up whoever had a hand in making this, to begin with."

"I made it, myself," she said. "Just me. And I delivered it."

* * *

Atep banished everyone from the room but his assistants, and the guards at the door wouldn't let her back in. Though it seemed that hours passed, the truth saw less than an hour's jump on the sundial before Atep arrived at her door. Within minutes, she was standing in front of the tomato plants on the outskirts of the flower garden.

"But they're not poisonous!" she insisted again. The stubborn physician wouldn't listen to her. Snatching a fruit from its vine, she took a large bite. "See?" She chewed and swallowed. "I tell you, I ate one of these last night. Nothing will happen. They're delicious."

Atep looked to the guardsmen who'd accompanied them. "I want a test. Give one of these to every creature you can locate. Force it down their throats, if necessary."

"The beef." Jayna grasped Atep's arm. "Maybe the beef turned. It had been sitting out awhile."

"Maybe," Atep said doubtfully. "Join me in the kitchen, please."

When they arrived, Marijani was taking down the amphorae, spreading the jars and bowls around the table as they'd been the night past. Jayna caught her pitying gaze, and her heart gave a painful twist. No one this morning had looked at her with anything less than condemnation. Pity was a welcome respite.

She joined the woman, adding the familiar pottery to the growing collection on the table.

Suddenly, Marijani gasped. "You didn't use that!"

Jayna pulled her hand away from the narrow-necked earthenware jar as if stung. "Why?"

She glanced at Atep as he stepped near to inspect the contents of the jar.

"It's larkspur seed, Your Highness. It's deadly."

Horror rushed through Jayna. Larkspur. The flower from her wedding.

This *spice* had been the final ingredient she'd used before judging her sauce ready. "It was on the table," she said.

Marijani shook her head. "Your Highness, I'm sorry to differ, but I didn't put it there. I wouldn't put it there. It's not meant for any table."

"Then why was it here last night?"

The woman glanced at the imperious healer and the host of guards before she looked at Jayna. "It wasn't. I mean, I didn't put it there. Do you remember me putting it there?" Her tongue passed nervously over her lips. "Please think. I would never put such a thing on a table made for food."

Jayna retraced the night in her mind. For the life of her, she couldn't distinctly remember seeing the woman place the jar on the table.

Marijani looked at the larkspur seed with horror. "I wouldn't make a mistake like that. I've worked in kitchens all my life. I know what I'm doing. Please, believe me. I would never harm the Pharaoh. Or Yourself. I pray you believe me."

Jayna looked into the woman's brown eyes and found no guile. She was scared, yes, but there was nothing there to dub her a traitor.

So how had the jar of larkspur found its way onto the table?

The swatches of cloth. She'd followed Orisa out of the room, leaving the kitchen unattended.

Jayna put her hand to her head. There were two entrances to the kitchen. Had one of the group snuck in while she was gone and placed the larkspur underhand?

With a force of will she hadn't realized she possessed, she grasped the woman's hand. "I believe you. I know you didn't do it."

"I've got to get back to my patient." Atep shoved the jar at Marijani. "Get this out of the kitchen and don't allow it back in."

Jayna turned and followed after the healer, racing to catch up with him. "Is it bad, Atep? Will it kill him?"

Dark eyes slanted down at her for the briefest second. "Time will tell."

Jayna stopped at his grim tone.

The man continued on down the corridor at breakneck speed. She watched him round the corner, then realized her closest link to Amony would soon disappear behind the chamber door. Hiking up her gown, she ran after him.

"Atep!" She caught him half-way to the royal quarters. "Can I see him?"

"No."

"How is he? Is he conscious? Is he hurting?"

The healer remained silent, chilling her.

"Tell him I want to see him—"

He pushed through the door, leaving her standing alone in the hallway. She stood there for several minutes, then turned to go to her chamber.

Was the group responsible for the jar of poison being on the table? Had they tried to kill her and hurt Amony instead? That surely wouldn't displease them, but—why would they want her dead?

She wasn't ready to think about it. The knowledge that the man she loved lay sick and possibly dying in the very bed in which they'd made love only hours ago was more than she could bear.

She walked slowly toward her chamber. Mamo waited outside, fidgeting the way he always did. He held his hands out to her. Jayna received another statuette. This one was of herself in a full, flowing robe.

"It's beautiful, Mam—"

Turning the slim stone over in her palm, she froze. Where flowing hair should have cascaded down the figurine's back, another face was carved, just like hers, identical to the other side. The statuette had two faces.

She raised her gaze to Mamo. His dark eyes watched her intently, almost cautiously, then he smiled, a slight, almost fearful smile.

"It's beautiful, Mamo," she said through stiffened lips. "Thank you."

The man's head bobbed, then he shuffled away down the corridor.

Stunned, Jayna backed through her door and into her chamber.

***

Atep sent a messenger out occasionally. Amony had been purged of the poison and was fighting what had already spread through his system. He was conscious but having difficulty breathing.

Jayna stayed in her chamber, receiving what news there was to be had through a servant. Night brought a mixture of dreams—the angry, grieving sister; the woman in love with the Pharaoh who took her fishing. From afar, Jayna watched and marveled that the dream-woman she observed was her brown-eyed self. Then the woman walked toward her from a calm, blue pond, calling her name, and Jayna stepped back. The woman halted, as if sensing her worry, then turned around. An identical face showed where the back of her head should have been, except her eyes were green, not brown. The queen's face. Her face. And in her hands, she clutched the hilt of a knife, the point dripping red with blood.

Jayna woke with a gasp, her whole body trembling.

Mamo's statuette! she thought, knowing the stone figure had caused the nightmare. But what did it mean?

Curling into a ball, she pulled her sheet over her head.

The frightening image of the bloody knife wouldn't fade.

Chapter Twenty

Broaching Tiy on the matter of the poisoning proved impossible. The ramifications were huge, and she wasn't up to facing huge just yet. She didn't eat. She had no appetite. So while she could rest easy on her fear of another poisoning attempt, she wondered if, as with Amony, danger lurked around every corner.

By morning the court received word that the Pharaoh was out of jeopardy. Jayna asked immediately to be let in. She was denied. Retreating to the dining room, she ate a bit of lunch from the platters three other women were sampling, and stayed with the general assembly of court hangers-on. By afternoon she counted no less than eight people who'd been admitted to see Amony, and still she was denied.

"Why?" she asked after demanding to speak to Atep. The healer blocked the door while a stout guard flanked each side. "Have you told him I want to see him? Is he denying me, or are you?"

"The Pharaoh is choosing his visitors."

"I don't believe you."

"I wouldn't lie."

"You've told him I want to see him?"

"Yes. He's not ready to receive you, yet. I'll send a messenger for you when he gives the word."

"Fine." Jayna glared at him, then dropped her gaze to the floor. Tears came again. "Tell him I'm thinking of him," she said through her tightening throat. "Tell him I need to see him. Please? Tell him that."

"I'll inform him."

She couldn't meet the man's gaze. "Thank you."

Turning away, she realized the door was opening again. She wheeled around. Had Amony decided to see her?

Roble stepped out.

Disappointment twisted deep in her chest.

"You look upset," he said. "I hear the Pharaoh hasn't allowed you in. Understandable, given you were the bearer of his poison—*pizza*—was the word?"

Jayna glanced away.

"There's been a great push to seek out the culprit," he said. "Your name is mentioned to calm a needless investigation, I believe. I can't tell you what position you're in at present."

Moistening her lips, Jayna said, "The unusual thing about the poisoning is that I made the pizza for myself." She watched his facial expression closely. "I didn't intend on sharing it with Amony, or anyone."

"Hmm," he murmured. "Perhaps you should stay out of the kitchen."

***

A short time later, the head of the king's guard arrived at Jayna's chamber. "Your Highness, Yera requests your presence in the council room."

Jayna's flesh tingled at mention of the vizier. She looked to her ladies. Orisa's dark eyes went wide with fear.

"For what, good guard?" Jayna asked, returning her attention to the man.

"Questions must be answered, Your Highness."

"Give me a moment—"

"I'm sorry, Your Highness, but I was directed to collect you immediately."

The ladies closed in behind her. Jayna stood stiff. "I haven't even time to change my clothes?"

The guard had the decency to look uncomfortable. "No, Your Highness. You must come now."

Jayna felt hands upon her back and shoulders, her ladies offering comfort and strength. She turned to them. "I'll return shortly."

Penda stretched forth a hand. And Maisha. And Orisa. And Naja. Jayna kissed all her ladies upon the cheek and drew courage from the murmurs and hugs she received in return. Yera, her enemy, her judge, awaited her in the council room, and she looked guilty as sin.

She followed the guard, and discovered that no less than six stout others waited outside her door, their eyes trained on her as if she'd flee. They reached the council room and, stepping inside, Jayna looked around in disbelief. An entire crowd had assembled. All the nobles currently in residence at the palace were present, seated in the chairs that dominated the sides of the room. She searched their faces and found every member of the group in attendance.

Deep within the room, Yera sat in a chair upon a raised dais. Amony's seat.

The guard escorted her to a small circle of tiles ten feet from the dais, then retreated. She stood alone, facing the man she believed to be her brother's killer, and around her sat the nobles who longed for her husband's death.

"Your Highness." Yera smiled with a pity far different from what Marijani had displayed. His pity was that of a scorpion with its tail poised to sting. "The court has questions surrounding the Pharaoh's poisoning. I apologize. These proceedings are difficult—"

"I understand." In her hatred for the man, Jayna's voice carried strong and true. "If you have questions for me, ask them."

Yera covered his surprise well, but not his malice. He wasted not a second in observing dryly, and loudly: "Larkspur seed. Interesting. Wasn't larkspur the flower of choice at your wedding to the Pharaoh?"

Jayna resented answering, but knew she had to. She said simply, "Yes."

The vizier's face grew serious, his seeming attempt at lightness barely a memory. "Did you take food to the Pharaoh late last night?"

"Yes," she said, again. "I told Atep that I did."

"Did you know it contained poison?"

"Not at the time."

"Your Highness." Yera bowed his head. "Servants will testify that you've visited the Pharaoh's chambers less than a handful of times in your marriage, and never for more than a minute or two. What was your purpose to be there last night?"

"To share a light repast," Jayna said.

"In bed? You shared the Pharaoh's bed?"

Highly aware that members of her diabolical group were watching and listening, Jayna murmured, "As it turned out."

Yera leaned forward. "Are you aware that blood was found on the Pharaoh's sheets?"

Jayna's heart stalled. "No."

"A small trace of blood—evidently not the Pharaoh's—was found in his bed. Can it be that you, too, were harmed in some way last night?"

"I—wasn't harmed," Jayna said. She'd been a virgin. Could the blood have been her virgin blood? With some embarrassment, she offered the closest thing to the truth that she felt she could afford. "My cycle is upon me."

Dark eyes watched her closely.

"The connection between your unusual, and untypical, length of stay in your husband's chamber, and this attempt on his life, comes at a most coincidental time. Had you some idea that the Pharaoh would force you to remain with him on this occasion?"

Frowning, she shook her head. "No."

"It's difficult not to connect the two—your unusual presence in his chamber and his poisoning."

What could she say? "It was only coincidence."

Yera fired back a question. "Did you spend the night with your husband, then leave before dawn?"

"Yes."

"Did you speak to him, or he to you, before you left his chamber?"

"No."

"You just left?"

Regret gripped Jayna's heart like a heavy fist. If only she'd known that the poison had been working its hazards on him when she'd looked into his still face. "He was sleeping," she said. "I didn't want to disturb him."

"Were you in the bed beside him while he slept?"

"Yes," she said, guilt threatening to overwhelm her.

"And you didn't hear a thing?" Yera's voice was rich with doubt. "He didn't say he wasn't feeling well? He didn't twist about or clutch his abdomen?"

"No."

"Atep has already testified that the poison in question would produce effects such as I've just named."

Guilt tore through Jayna in ever-widening ripples. Had he called for her? Tried to wake her? With the type of dreams she'd been having, could she have slept through his cries for help?

"Your Highness." Yera's voice rose in command. "Did you enter the Pharaoh's chamber last night, seduce him with a poisoned meal, then leave him to die?"

"I certainly did not!" she cried.

"Your Highness, did you make a mystery visit to your mother recently?"

The question surprised her. She shook her head. "My visit had no mystery about it."

"Does your mother have some grudge against our Pharaoh?"

A prickle of alarm ran up her spine. "What does my mother have to do with this?"

"The court needs to determine if one woman's hysteria could bring about another woman's action."

Dread settled in Jayna's chest. "What are you saying?"

"Did you and your mother, a woman who fled the country for her ravings against the Pharaoh, conspire to poison your husband?"

"Is that what you're telling him?" she asked, her lungs struggling suddenly to draw air. "Are you telling him these stories? No wonder—"

Yera urged, "Yes? Finish, please."

"No wonder he won't see me!" Her words spilled from her, despite her better judgment. "Are you bringing charges against me?" she demanded.

"The Pharaoh lives," Yera said. "It's his decision."

"Then I want to see him. Why isn't he here?"

"These proceedings will be relayed to him in detail."

Anger twisted through Jayna. "I demand to speak with him. If you're not going to arrest me, I want to speak to him!"

"That's not possible."

Jayna stepped out of the dias' circle. "Join me, if you wish, but I will speak with him."

She turned and walked back through the room. The flurry around her, and the sound of sandals on the tiles told her she had substantial accompaniment, which was good, because she wasn't sure she'd get in to see Amony without some heavy backing.

The guard, seeing the host of them approaching, Jayna at the lead, stretched forth an arm, but she shoved past him and pushed through the door.

Amony sat in a chair in the nearer portion of the room.

The sight of him sent a wave of emotion surging through her. Handsome and dynamic, he was dressed in a light robe of deep-russet, his black hair brushing the top of the collar. He held a papyrus in one hand, his other arm rested on the small table. Two of his advisors sat across the table from him. They all looked up as she entered the room.

"Amony."

His face was pale, and dark circles underscored his eyes. He looked wonderful, and terrible.

She dropped to her knees beside him and put her hand on the robe that covered his thigh. She didn't have to look behind her to know the conspiratiors stood only a foot away amongst the others. She didn't care.

"I'm so sorry," she said. "Has it been awful?"

No answer came forth. He just looked at her, his face unchanging, unsmiling.

"I didn't mean it," she said. "You've got to know I didn't mean it."

"I'm not pursuing punishment."

"You're not—" She drew back. Looking into his expressionless eyes, she shook her head. "So you don't think I did it?"

He didn't speak, nor move, only stared at her.

"You *do* think I did it?"

His silence spoke volumes. She pushed to her feet in dismay.

He wasn't going to punish her, but he believed her guilty?

Was it the larkspur? Had the fact that the poison was larkspur seed proved her guilty in his mind? What else could it be? He trusted her now. Or he *had* trusted her.

If only it had been any other toxin but that one!

Dark, cool eyes stared blankly at her.

Had their night in his bed saved her from his wrath, just as it was *alleged* to have led to his death? Incredibly, he believed that lie. But he believed, too, the passion they'd shared in each other's arms.

She wouldn't back down to the lie. The entire group stood witness, but she didn't care. The trial had likely damaged her standing with them beyond repair. She wanted more from her husband! She wanted his trust. His love. Leaning over, she kissed him on the lips, a soft touching that contained her heart.

He sat motionless, not responding.

She straightened.

His gaze moved away. He wouldn't look at her.

Tears sprang to her eyes. She was on the outside again. He wasn't seeking her punishment, but neither did he believe her. Or forgive her.

She whirled. Shoving through the guards, past Yera and Roble and Tiy, she raced out of her husband's chamber.

Chapter Twenty-One

"What is it, Your Highness? Where are you going? Your Highness, you can't just go off like this. Your Highness! Jayna!"

Hearing her name made Jayna stop just short of the palace gates. Orisa hurried toward her. "Where are you going? You're upset."

"You're right, I'm upset. I've got to get out of this palace for a while and think. This place is clogging my brain."

She resumed walking, and Orisa followed.

"Where do you plan to go?"

"I don't know. Away." She gestured to the streets and buildings ahead. "Into the city."

"On your own? I can't allow it."

"I'm going, Orisa."

"You need a guard. Three or four men—" She waved her urgency toward the gate sentry.

"No!" Jayna tugged at her cousin's arm. "I don't want any reminders of who I am right now. I need—" Pain twisted in her chest. She splayed her fingers out, and willed her breathing to slow. "I need some time just not being queen."

"Everyone knows you. Your fine jewels and clothes will give you away at first sight. You can't run."

"Then I'll remove them." Slipping her bracelets off her arms, Jayna tucked them in her pocket.

"And your gown?"

Jayna stopped and glanced down at herself. The guard hadn't allowed her to change before the questioning. Despite what Orisa thought, her gown could definitely be found lacking. Reaching back, she unfastened her weighty necklace. She handed the necklace to her cousin.

"What will you do once you're there?"

Jayna hesitated. "I don't know."

"I have an idea," Orisa said slowly, wariness in her eyes. "If you'll take me with you. The Festival of Horus is upon us. The eastern district always has a huge celebration with music, and dancing in the streets."

The idea appealed to Jayna. "That sounds perfect. It would be quite an education, if nothing else."

As Orisa stripped off the more valuable pieces of her jewelry, a royal chariot drew around the palace gate and rumbled to a stop beside them.

Jayna closed her eyes and moaned. Would she be prevented from walking any farther from the palace?

"Let the guard follow us," Orisa implored. "We can have him stay back where he won't be seen. He'll be there for us only if we need him."

Perking, Jayna nodded. Her relief at not being denied her freedom was so great she would have allowed a dozen guards.

Now that her course was truly set, her spirit lightened. A night on the town as her simple, unroyal self would be just the thing to get her thoughts together. As much as she wished to be passing the evening in Amony's chamber with his favor upon her, she looked forward to this adventure. She needed some time away from the palace and Amony's potent presence. She needed to collect her emotions.

Torches threw an orange light over the sector of town where the festivities were taking place. The glow against the black night sky showed them the way. Music and laughter reached their ears long before Jayna and Orisa arrived on the outer fringe. The guard and chariot halted at a discreet distance.

People packed the center of the street, their bodies gyrating as they danced to a lively tune. Musicians played loudly from a raised platform at the far end of the row of buildings. Jayna and Orisa stayed along the side and strolled past tables of food and drink. Groups formed all along the strip, people talking and laughing, enjoying the refreshments.

"This could be fun," Jayna said.

"As long as we're left alone."

Orisa sounded worried, and Jayna followed her cousin's gaze. A pair of oversized villagers eyed them closely, then started toward them. Jayna leaned near Orisa. "We could tell them we're expecting our big boyfriends—as soon as they're done wrestling the lion we ran into on our way here."

Her comment drew a giggle from Orisa which her cousin quickly squelched. With a frown, she yanked Jayna quickly back along the way they'd come, stopping abruptly at one of the tables. "Let's get a—" She looked over the table's offering. "Oh!" Freshly-poured cups of wine covered the surface, the only bounty available.

This time, Jayna chuckled. She picked up a cup. "I believe I will."

Orisa frowned at her. "You'll not get drunk on me tonight."

"Says who?"

Her cousin grasped her arm. "Nothing good will come of losing your head."

Jayna shrugged. "My head, my heart..."

Orisa's face grew serious. "What happened?"

"I poisoned him, Orisa."

"Not you. You love him."

Jayna halted the cup at her lips and drew it back slowly. "Thank you."

"You don't have to thank me," Orisa said. "I know you love him."

Jayna clutched the cup tightly in her hands. "How do you know?"

"The way you look at him. The way you act with him."

"The way I—act?"

"The way you get so nervous sometimes. Relaxed at other times." She shook her head. "I don't know, but I can see it. Amony believes you, doesn't he? You're not here because something happened?"

"Something happened." Jayna took a drink from her cup, then met her cousin's gaze. "He thinks I poisoned him. Deliberately."

Orisa shook her head. "He couldn't."

"He does," Jayna said. "Though he's not pursuing punishment. *Official* punishment, that is." She drew a deep breath, and her eyes misted. "Not forgiving me, not returning my kiss, looking at me with dead eyes, this is his punishment. I suppose I should be thankful."

Orisa laid her hand on Jayna's arm. Jayna smiled at the comforting gesture.

"Your Highness." Another hand came upon her shoulder and she turned in surprise.

Nassor stood before her, his sleek hair slightly disheveled, his kilt impeccable. A single ring flashed from his right hand. He, too, must have removed his jewelry, for he was one given to an overabundance of adornment.

He glanced at Orisa. "I saw you two fleeing the palace," he said in hushed tones. "I couldn't believe my eyes when I saw you here."

"You followed us?" Jayna asked.

Nassor grasped her hand. "Only to assure myself of your safety."

"We brought a guard—"

"Born to do your bidding," he scoffed, "regardless of the consequences."

Jayna pulled her hand from the nobleman's. Such a flirt, she'd never met. No wonder Amony had come to her with such suspicion. "We're fine," she said. "You needn't stay around to look out for us."

"You're shooing me away," he pouted. "Well, not before we have a dance."

He grabbed her hands, and with a simple step backward, they were amongst the dancers. After a moment's consideration, Jayna held a finger up to Orisa, signaling how quickly she'd be back. Orisa nodded.

Nassor released her, his body swaying in front of her.

"Just one!" she said.

He smiled as she took up the rhythm, moving to the music with her arms and legs and hips. She loved dancing. She loved the wordless tunes that floated around her and made her move, made her feel. The damp heat in the air brought moisture to her skin. She closed her eyes and twirled around.

In her mind, she wasn't with Nassor anymore. She imagined Amony was the man she was dancing with. Her King. Her husband. She made herself believe it, and a smile came to her lips. She and Amony, dancing.

Yes. This time next year, at this festival. She would see to it that they came, and together they would dance. She'd spin, and she'd open her eyes, and he'd be there in front of her. It would happen. She'd look into the eyes of the man who wore fish as jewelry and couldn't keep his desire for her from shining through his eyes.

She completed another pirouette.

Nassor grinned back.

Not this year. Next year.

She glanced at Orisa. The tune was winding down, moving into another, but her cousin had joined the dance with a slim, good-looking man who smiled shyly at her.

Following her gaze, Nassor leaned forward. "Dance some more. You'll have to wait, anyway."

He made sense. She needed no further bidding. She'd caught the essence of the music, her husband, her place of belonging. Nassor didn't know it as she swayed away from him, but she danced for her husband, her lover. She danced for Amony, and for her future.

A long time later, Nassor led her back to the wine stand. Pressing a cup into her hands, he drank from his own. They sipped quietly, resting. Jayna watched Orisa and smiled at the happiness on her cousin's face as she danced with her new suitor.

A pair of women friends also stopped for a drink at the table. Jayna glanced over at them, then looked again. The lady farthest from her sported a swollen right eye ringed with a purplish-black bruise.

"Sudi wouldn't like this," the woman said. "He wouldn't like it at all."

"He's not here, is he?"

"Word may get to him." She took a quick drink from a cup.

"You don't even like him. Why does he keep coming around? Why don't you tell him to leave you alone?"

"You don't know him," the woman said. "He's insane."

"I know him," the other replied in dry tones. "What did you do this time? Glance at him?"

"I—"

The woman's gaze scanned the bystanders, so Jayna looked quickly away. But she listened intently.

"I don't know." The woman's voice lowered. "He flies into a rage over nothing. I don't know how he's survived this long without someone putting a knife into his belly."

"He's huge," the other said. "That's why. Whatever happened to Freno?"

"Sudi happened." The woman's voice cracked and nearly broke. "He won't come around with that beast threatening to gut him."

Jayna could stand no more. Stepping away from Nassor, she dug into her pocket and pulled out her bracelets. She pressed them into the surprised woman's hands. "Wait." Rushing out to Orisa, she demanded the return of her necklace which Orisa carried in the bag on her wrist. Cupping it discreetly, she stepped over to the woman.

Her back to the crowd, to Nassor, she whispered, "Take these. Just one of the bracelets could easily pay the price of a boat ride down-river to another town. The rest—well, their exchange would see you set until you find a living." She smiled. "Perhaps with Freno?"

The woman's mouth gaped open. "Are these—real?"

Jayna nodded. "They're real."

Nassor and Orisa joined her at the same time.

Jayna turned to her cousin. "Are you ready to go, or do you need more time?"

Orisa glanced aside to her new friend who stood watching her, a smile on his lips. She drew a deep breath. "I'm ready."

Jayna turned to Nassor. "Goodnight."

The nobleman looked confused. "Goodnight."

Jayna was quiet on the walk back, but her thoughts raced. Would the woman go to this Freno she'd spoken of? Given the valuables to start a new life, would she make her getaway, and take the man who cared for her? Jayna hoped she would. She hoped she'd been able to help the woman to that which she couldn't grasp in her own life.

Love.

A clear path to the man she loved.

Reality, staved off for the evening, crashed back in on her. She'd poisoned the man she was fighting to save. The thought of him dying, the very promise she'd read about in the tomb, ripped at her heart. He couldn't die. He couldn't. Not until he'd become a very old man with a full, rich life behind him. She had to stop the future from coming, a future that was fairly etched in stone, and make a new future for the man she loved.

Was it so impossible?

His queen loved him. She, Jayna Monroe, Great Royal Wife of the King of Egypt, loved her husband. There was no room in her heart or her mind to accept anything less.

And he loved her. He mistrusted her, but he loved her.

Jayna looked to the palace in the distance, and courage surged through her.

She would win him back. No longer would she torment in her heart over what she'd thought of him, or what she'd gone into this marriage planning to do. He was her husband, and she would go about this marriage of theirs with no doubts, no half-hearted gestures.

She'd helped the woman with the blackened eye tonight. She'd help herself, too.

Chapter Twenty-Two

Tiy strode into Jayna's chamber just as she lay down upon her bed. All but a single oil lamp had been put out, leaving a soft glow in this niche of the room. Jayna started to rise, but Tiy waved her back.

"Don't get up. You need your rest." She sat on the edge of the bed and looked down at her. "I can see you're weary. You can't take much more of this. It's become too much of a burden to champion your brother's death."

Alarm stiffened every muscle in Jayna's body. Acutely aware of her prone position, she watched Tiy warily. "I'm tired of the game, is all."

"You said, not too long ago, that you don't regard this as a game."

Jayna moistened her lips nervously. "It feels that way now, as it drags on."

Tiy nodded. "Yes, it does, because it's become one." Her brow raised pointedly. "You should have listened to me. I told you to take a lover, but you were already beyond that, weren't you? How long have you cared for him?"

Alarm gave way to full-blown panic. Jayna couldn't meet her gaze. "Cared for whom?"

"For your husband," Tiy spoke each word clearly. "The man whose bed you left your virgin blood in the night before last."

The involuntary act of drawing air into her lungs became a chore Jayna could barely manage. "You don't know what happened."

"He forced you," Tiy drawled with sarcasm. "You took him a simple repast to lull him into a false security, never thinking he might be ready for bed, and ready to have you in it." She swung her hand in dismissal. "Whatever your story, the result is the same. You care for him, and you'll try to spare him his fate."

Jayna sat up. "I served him a poisoned meal—"

"I served *you* a poisoned meal."

Though she had suspicions aplenty, the outright confession shocked her. "It was you?"

Tiy shrugged. "You wouldn't have died. Neither would he. You might never have been the same again, had you ate as much as our mighty Pharaoh, but your appetite is limited these days, isn't it?"

Jayna shook her head. "Why?"

The woman's brows rose in question. "Why did I substitute your ingredients? I would have liked to do so for Amony on previous occasions—I thank you for the unexpected pleasure—but that kitchen is like a box of scorpions."

Affection for Marijani grew tenfold in Jayna's heart.

"None of us can get near it," Tiy lamented, "and serving up a dish for Amony, alone, has posed more dilemmas than I've been able to out-think." The older woman sighed. "From the beginning, I knew you weren't what you pretended to be. Your rage was impressive, but I couldn't see any woman throwing away her life for what you planned."

Jayna frowned. "What do you mean?"

"To live in exile for the rest of your life with a man you hate?" the woman queried, dubious. "Granted, you would surely have soon been a widow. The Great Pharaoh Amony would fight for his throne, no matter that it would be a losing battle. Sefu will never let it go, and neither will I."

"Sefu? And you?"

"We will rule! Do not doubt us!"

A jolt shot through Jayna's chest, mushrooming with an intensity that made her blood rush faster and her thoughts race. Sefu and Tiy as King and Queen? She and Amony living out their lives together?

Tiy's mouth twisted in a scowl. "You never showed the dedication to our cause that I thought you should. I told the group that, too, more than once. They believed in you, but I knew you."

Joy exploded inside Jayna. Joy and relief. She hadn't meant to kill Amony at all! She'd even married him with the knowledge she'd be bound to him ever after.

She turned her face away, groping with the incredible revelation, fighting to control any reaction that might further give her away. She had to try to fool Tiy, no matter the damaging evidence.

"You're right," she said, fighting to keep her voice level. "I should have taken a lover. But you're wrong in thinking my heart is anywhere but with the group."

"You lie!"

Before Jayna could do more than flinch, Tiy shoved a knife to her throat.

"What—"

"Silence!" Tiy hissed through clenched teeth. "You'll close your mouth, and you'll keep it closed. Do you understand me?"

She jerked the knife away—and up. Pain seared Jayna's temple. Crying out, she clutched a hand to the spot. Wet warmth oozed through her fingers. Raising her stunned gaze, she looked at the woman who stood looking down at her, the tip of her dagger red with blood.

"You'll stay quiet. Worse will descend upon you, more than you can bear, if you don't keep your tongue in your mouth."

Leaning forward, she wiped the blade against Jayna's silk sheet. With a final, cold glance, she turned and left the room.

Jayna pulled her hand away from her temple and looked at the dark blood that covered her palm and ran a brighter red over her fingers. She left her bed and crossed the room on trembling legs. Pulling open a drawer, she retrieved a cloth and pressed it to the cut.

Fear hammered inside her chest.

She picked up her hand mirror, and took it over to the light. Sitting on her bed, she pulled the cloth back.

Her missing scar.

She'd just received the injury whose presence she'd carried her whole life, but had lost upon coming here. The scar she'd been born with.

She dropped the mirror and reapplied the cloth.

Was this how she'd gotten the scar? Had this injury carried itself four thousand years into the present?

With an impending sense of doom, she considered the meaning of acquiring the scar now.

Had she, as queen, backed down in this moment and let it become the turning point where the future became what it had: Amony dead and she known throughout time as the woman who'd killed him?

She and the queen. One and the same.

She closed her eyes.

Was it over? Had the end come?

The end for whom? For her? For Amony? For both of them?

The cut which would surely scar into her future told her to run, and run fast. She had to tell Amony what she knew *now*.

Throwing the cloth on the table, she ran across her room, out the door, and down the corridor to his chamber. Even his stalwart guard would not stop her.

"He's not here." The man's words halted her.

"Where is he?"

"In the council room."

"Thank you." Jayna whirled and headed back, past her room, toward the front of the palace. Sure enough, lights blazed from every corner, and voices carried out to her.

Roble's voice. And Amony's.

"She named Mamo."

"You're certain she meant no one else?"

"'Mamo', she said. Over and over. 'Mamo did' was all she could manage, the poor thing. Her lips are swollen and cut nearly as much as her eyes."

Jayna stopped at the threshold of the room. Two guards held Mamo's arms. Roble and Hareb stood in front of Amony.

Amony ran a hand through his hair. "He's never displayed such a temperament around the palace."

"He beat the girl bloody," Hareb said. "We hope she'll make it through the night."

Jayna walked toward them, stunned. "Mamo wouldn't hurt a wasp." She looked into the man-child's frightened eyes. "Whatever happened to the girl, Mamo didn't do it."

"Maybe he didn't," Roble said. "She named him, but she's out of her mind with pain. We'll have to see what she says when she recovers. In the meantime, Your Highness," he addressed Amony, "for the safety of the other young women in this kingdom, we must detain him."

"Of course," Amony said.

Glancing at Roble, Jayna realized he looked at her steadily, as if waiting for the touch of her gaze. Triumph flashed in his eyes before he turned to Amony. "My wife fears the girl may have been raped, as well. Knowing this is a capital offense, we don't mean to accuse but, Your Highness is, at least, prepared for all the possibilities." Roble looked at Jayna again. "Time will tell. As the girl recovers, we'll be able to learn just how serious the charges need be."

An icy chill ran through Jayna as Roble delivered her message. Keep quiet to Amony about the plot. A wrong word from her would surely turn the woman's mutterings into a full, coherent accusation. Were they so certain Amony wouldn't simply listen to her, then arrest them all before they could hurt Mamo?

Your Highness, the Queen is only trying to shift guilt away from herself for her poisoning of you.

She wants to cast doubt in your mind about all of us, that she may look better in your eyes.

You'd believe the woman who already tried to kill you, Your Highness?

The poison was larkspur, Your Highness. Larkspur!

They had to have some doubt, else Tiy wouldn't have cut her and warned her. If they completely believed Amony would ignore her story, they wouldn't go to such lengths to frame Mamo.

But if she told him what she knew, and he didn't react positively, and quickly? Mamo would die for a rape he didn't commit. Then Amony would die.

She didn't care about herself anymore. Obviously they knew that. But she did care about Mamo. This, too, they knew. And she loved Amony with her entire heart and soul. Had Tiy convinced them? She must have for this elaborate scheme to be taking place.

She watched the guards lead Mamo away, her heart aching. He looked so frightened. So helpless. If only she could speak and end this madness! But she couldn't. Could she?

Laughter echoed in her ears. Roble's incredulous laugh and pointed finger. Hareb shaking his head in disbelief. *Larkspur, Your Highness.*

The degree of her guilt in the plot, or the lack of her guilt, no longer mattered. They'd made her the villain, and Amony could do nothing but believe them over her.

She brushed at her cheekbone, and her hand came away wet. She looked down. A drop of blood had trickled down from the cut on her temple.

"You ought to have someone take a look at that."

Jayna looked up to see Roble standing in front of her. He smiled. "I can send Tiy around."

Twisting, Jayna ran from the room. Rounding the corridor that led to her chamber, she fell straight into Nassor's arms.

"What is it?" the man asked, his gaze moving over her face. "You look terrible. Something has happened."

"It's Mamo!" she cried. "He's been arrested for assaulting a woman."

"No!" he said in disbelief. Then added, "I'm sorry."

Jayna wiped her cheek. This time, it was tears that fell. "Me, too." She sniffed heavily. "I've got to go."

"Where?"

"My chamber."

"I think you need to talk."

"No." She shook her head and sniffed again. "I don't need to talk. I can't talk. I need to be quiet. Very quiet."

She left him, a dumbfounded expression on his face, and went to her chamber. Her ladies started to enter from their chamber, and she told them to leave. She threw herself onto the bed and buried her head in the cushions.

Oh, Mamo! Amony!

She couldn't have either man's death on her conscience. Good Lord, did she already? An insignificant man like Mamo wouldn't warrant a place in the writings of the tomb of a Pharaoh. Had sweet, innocent Mamo died in this whole thing?

Jayna groaned and cried out loud, muffling the sounds of her anguish in her silken cushions.

Chapter Twenty-Three

Mamo's condition was far better than she'd feared. The group had framed him, but they obviously didn't mean to make him suffer too much—barring, of course, the threat of death that hung over his head. She prayed he didn't realize the full extent of his situation.

Arriving at the damp, dark jail, she found him sitting on a plump-looking cot, happily carving, a pursuit none of the other prisoners would have been allowed for the sharpness of the necessary instruments. A full platter of food and a large mug rested on a small table at the head of his cot.

"What is this?" she asked the guard of his comfortable surroundings.

The guard had no trouble understanding what she meant. "The Pharaoh's orders."

"He can do that?"

The guard looked at her in surprise. "Of course." He pulled back the barred door and let her in.

Mamo rose to greet her. Her heart wrenched when he squeezed the hands she held out to him.

"How are you, Mamo?"

His soft smile encouraged her.

"You'll be out soon, you know that? We miss you."

They talked for awhile, and Mamo showed her his newest project. Jayna promised to visit him every day, then left, guilt dogging her every step.

***

Amidst the gossip surrounding her, the curious, sometimes harsh gazes she received were unpleasant but understandable. In the space of a few days, she'd been blamed for poisoning the Pharaoh and had lost a dear friend to the heinous accusation of battering an innocent woman. Unfortunately, popular reaction to her seemed to only grow worse.

She allowed Nassor to accompany her to the terrace for an afternoon break by the pool, and went to sit with Edet and Kessie, as planned. It seemed as though all eyes followed them across the terrace.

"Your Highness," Edet said, rising as she and Nassor sat. "If you'll excuse us, we were just leaving."

His flustered-looking wife resisted.

"Come, dear," he said, his hand at her elbow.

"I must speak to her."

"Come!" her husband ordered.

Jayna stood as the woman did. "What troubles you, Kessie?" Her friend looked to be in genuine distress. "What did you want to say?"

"Perhaps a more private time would be better."

"No," Jayna said, worried for the woman. "Talk to me now. What is it?"

"Please—" Kessie looked to her husband, then stepped out of his grasp. Placing her back to the table, she spoke low. "I just want you to know I don't believe what they're saying. I know you love your husband. If—if you need someone to talk to, I want you to know that I'm always available. Sometimes," she threw a quick glance over her shoulder at Nassor, "a woman's ear can be as kind as a man's, and her shoulder just as strong for crying on."

"Kessie!"

Kessie ignored her husband as her gaze moved to the tall man who stepped out of the terrace's archway. Amony. Jayna watched her husband with longing. The Pharaoh had joined his nobles for the afternoon reprieve.

"I'll stay with you," Kessie said, dodging her husband's grasp again. "The Pharaoh need not think a thing of this gathering with myself present."

Jayna frowned, her blood charged with anxiety over a matter she scarcely understood. "What do you mean? Why would he think anything amiss?"

"You don't know what they're saying?"

A strange prickling crawled over Jayna's skin, a foreboding that made her shiver. "What are they saying?"

Compassion warmed Kessie's eyes. "That you're dallying with another man." Her gaze returned to the handsome man seated at the table. "Probably Nassor."

The revelation wasn't what she'd expected. No deadly secrets spilled from the group members. Then, with a jolt, she remembered Amony's reasoning for coming to the house in Saqqara. He was already jealous of the nobleman.

"Has the Pharaoh heard this?" she asked.

"I can't imagine that he hasn't," Kessie said. "It's on everyone's lips."

Jayna stood still, feeling as if the very sky was closing in on her, determined to squash her. Amony already believed she'd poisoned him. How much more distant could his heart be from a wife who was unfaithful to him? How less credible any word she spoke, much less an accusation of treachery toward his inner circle? The conspirators *were* involved in this rumor. They'd started it to discredit her in Amony's eyes, of that she was certain.

Biting back a groan, she squeezed her friend's hand. "Thank you, Kessie. For everything. Go with your husband for now." She stepped over to Nassor. "I must join my husband."

Leaving him with the simple explanation, she made her way across the terrace to where Amony joined a table of nobles. None of the conspirators were in direct attendance. The closest of the group was Hareb who sat one table away, apparently not at all interested in what went on around him. Jayna thought his nonchalance a bit obvious when her every move was watched, at least covertly, by every member of court.

Two chairs remained open at Amony's table, encouraging her. She stepped forward, her gaze on Amony. He wore a blue-and-white striped kilt today, and a thick bronze necklace that rested heavy-looking on his powerful, sun-burnished chest.

"Your Highness." She waited for the touch of his gaze the way another woman would await her lover's caress.

The dark eyes turned to her.

"May I sit with you?" she asked, desperate to hear the sound of his low, rich voice.

"This is a private discussion." His flat tone thrust through her heart like a dagger.

He looked away.

He didn't want her with him.

He believed the rumors.

Feeling the gazes of his tablemates upon her, she steeled her expression, unwilling to let them see her pain.

"Excuse me, Your Highness." Her voice came out in a waver as she forced his attention upon her again. His gaze moved coolly over her. She cleared her suddenly clogged throat. "Perhaps we can talk later?"

"I'll make no promises." With that he turned his back on her.

Jayna stiffened. The urge to pull him back around to face her hit her heavily. She wanted to grab that handsome head and make him look her in the eye. She wanted to demand they go to his chamber and talk it out.

She couldn't force him, though. He was hurt. He didn't believe in her, and she should count herself fortunate that he hadn't thrown her in jail, or already had her executed for her poisoning of him.

She turned and walked toward the archway with as much dignity as she could muster, but she felt more like a frightened scorpion retreating before the hateful eyes and threatening heels of the court.

Why hadn't Amony punished her in a more substantial way? Why wasn't she sharing a cell with Mamo? Was he only awaiting rock-hard proof of her treachery?

How long before the group provided him with that?

Why didn't they just kill her off?

The reasoning came immediately.

Two dead royals in a short amount of time would look suspicious. They had to let her live until they could get rid of Amony. Then, she knew, they'd deal with her.

Chapter Twenty-Four

Jayna opened her eyes slowly and looked into Maisha's face. Her makeup was complete, her headache from her horrible night's sleep finally gone.

"Shall we accompany you, Your Highness?"

"Yes." She didn't want to be alone.

"Let's be on our way, then," Penda said with forced cheer. "We'll be right on time."

Jayna had to attend the public lunch. Evasive as Amony had become, he'd been present yesterday, and she, expecting a repeat of his absence, had hid away in her chamber. She had to see him, and let him see her. Their marriage was dissolving, again, into a relationship of ghosts.

The queen and her ladies walked to the dining hall, a solemn group in the watchful, whispering court. Jayna's gaze scanned the hall. The Pharaoh's regal head bent in conversation at one of the men's tables. A start of excitement and nervousness charged Jayna's breast. *He's here!*

Two long days since his rejection of her, and finally she shared the same room with him. She could hardly place one foot properly in front of the other. What if he looked up and saw her? He might notice her walking across the room. His gaze might touch her. What would he think? What would he feel, looking upon her?

Reaching her table with relief, she sat down in a vacant chair. The sight of meat and fruit piled high on platters sent a wave of nausea through her. Her stomach would hold no food today.

She looked away.

Her gaze caught on Tiy and Sefu as they strode into the room, their arms linked, wide smiles on both their faces. The future King and Queen?

With distaste, she watched the two separate. Sefu stopped at Amony's elbow and spoke a few words. He appeared very confident, this man who would see the Pharaoh dead and the throne his own.

Her thinking had been only slightly off. Sefu, not Yera, aimed for the throne of Egypt. Yera was content as vizier, under the proper King. Without doubt, Sefu would make just the sort of dishonorable king he desired.

Loathing rose inside her, her anger for the senseless loss of her brother choking her. Two men now held her utter hatred, two men whose hands were stained with her brother's blood. As her mother had said, a Pharaoh is his vizier, as much as a vizier is his Pharaoh. Sefu was every bit as guilty as Yera, and Yera was as guilty as Sefu.

She dragged her gaze away from the hateful men, and looked to the woman who would be Queen. Tiy. The woman smiled—no, she beamed—at Rana and Desta. All the women looked very happy, as delighted and full of themselves as...

Jayna glanced back to Sefu.

...as Sefu was confident and proud.

Jayna's heart lurched. She'd seen this all before. The group had hatched a new plan!

Chapter Twenty-Five

Pacing the corridor outside the council room, Jayna agonized that, for the first time, she had no idea what the group had plotted for her husband. They certainly hadn't included her in the discussion.

What is it? she thought for the hundredth time. *Oh, God, what is it?*

One thing was certain. She wasn't going to spend a single moment far from Amony's side.

Reaching the intersection of corridors, she turned. Amony was holding court in his council room. She had to stay near the council room.

No deed not fully explainable would affect her husband without her there to observe it and halt it, if need be.

Chapter Twenty-Six

Sleep was of no consequence. Her nerves stretched so tight, she wouldn't have been able to rest, anyway. Just how long she could keep up her nocturnal vigil outside Amony's bedchamber, however, didn't require addressing. The first morning's dawn brought a young man at a full run. Jayna stepped behind the wall, unwilling to let anyone but Amony's guards ponder the reason for her presence, and peered at him from around the corner. Dressed in a coarse linen kilt and tattered brown sandals, the man skidded to a halt in front of Amony's door.

"I bring a message to the Pharaoh from his noble, Sefu. It's urgent."

The guard stepped inside the reception room, leaving the man alone. Jayna ducked as the fellow's face turned her way, then she carefully peeked out again. The messenger was looking the other way down the corridor, now. His slim shoulders relaxed suddenly, and he calmly brushed his hair from his eyes. Without warning, he resumed his tense stance and she could see a renewed expression of urgency on his face.

The guard stepped back into the hall. The young man went inside.

Jayna flattened against the wall, her heart thundering. He was faking! The urgent message from Sefu was false! Something was about to happen.

She had to find out what.

Drawing a deep breath, she stepped around the corner. This time she didn't pace past the guard, but walked directly to him. "I require an audience with my husband."

The guard nodded and stepped inside. A few moments later, he returned. "The Pharaoh apologizes. He's already in conference."

"I don't care," Jayna said. She would not be put off. "Tell my husband I need to speak with him immediately. *Immediately*," she emphasized.

A minute later, she was admitted into the reception room. The man who'd gone in before her waited in the corner. His head bowed respectfully when she entered, but she kept her gaze on the inner door. The guard stationed there swung the portal open for her.

Amony didn't look at her as his attendant secured his headdress. He allowed the man to complete the task, then nodded his dismissal.

"Are you going somewhere?" Jayna asked.

The side door closed behind the attendant.

Amony still didn't look at her. "Yes."

"Where?"

"About my duties."

"What duties?" Jayna asked. "Something concerning Sefu?"

The tension between them tore at her heart. His distant manner was worse than she ever remembered.

"If you must know," he said, finally meeting her gaze, "Sefu's laborers are rebelling. I'm going to settle the matter."

"Haven't I heard how strong-willed a master Sefu is?" Suspicion turned to cold, hard fact in Jayna's mind. "Suddenly he can't handle his people?"

"Thus the reason I'm going," Amony responded with reserve. "He's a strong leader. This can be nothing but a strong revolt."

Jayna shook her head. "Don't go. Just send your men. There's one in charge. He'll direct them."

Amony frowned, and he spoke gruffly, as if he resented speaking to her at all. "Sefu asked that I make a personal appearance. We must show great power."

His words sent warning bells off in her head. "The royal guard will do that very thing."

Her husband's dark brows furrowed deeper. "Why do you try to detain me?"

"Because—" She took a step forward, then another, and kept on going until she stood in front of him. Breathless with the need to speak, her heart twisting with fear, she opened her mouth.

The heat of his body reached out to her, and in that instant, his eyes flickered with the reddish-brown hue with which he'd regarded her in gentler moments.

She didn't realize what she did, even as she pulled his head down to hers and pressed her lips to his mouth.

She'd done it once before with disastrous results, but the horrible memory occurred to her when it was too late. She'd thrust herself upon him again, and he would reject her....

His hands gripped her upper arms.

Then his mouth slanted.

Ecstasy swept through her. Tears of joy sprang beneath her closed eyelids. He wanted her.

His fingers tensed on her arms, and he set her away from him. His chest rose and fell quickly, his eyes blazing with passion and confusion. He turned and strode toward the door.

"He's trying to kill you!" she blurted.

Amony stopped, his body stiffening.

She closed her eyes. "It's true. Sefu is trying to kill you. Along with Yera, and Tiy and Roble—"

Amony turned. "And you."

She couldn't keep the guilt from her face. To a degree, she was guilty. She wouldn't back down, though, not with Sefu drawing him away to his estate. Now was the time, no matter the repercussions.

She drew a shaky breath. "Though you may see me dead, I'm going to tell you the truth." Now was the time. "Sefu is trying to kill you." She moistened her lips. "He's trying to kill you, along with Yera, Tiy, Roble, Rana, Hareb and Desta. I know this, because I've sat in on their meetings. I—I only pretended to go along with them, so I could know what they intended and save you from it."

She fought to stand still as the muscular Pharaoh walked slowly toward her, closing the distance between them.

His face was stiff, his eyes dark and unreadable. "Why?"

"Because Sefu wants to be king."

His gaze searched her face. "You. Why are you a part of it?"

"I'm not," she said. "I entered into their group when they claimed only to want to unseat you. To discredit you. I went along with that because—" Could she admit to the reason?

"Because you think I killed your brother?"

He knew? She stared at him in surprise.

The corner of his mouth twisted with bitterness. "You think I didn't know about all the conjecture? The intrigue? Your mother? Her rantings are no secret to me. Throughout our courtship, I couldn't understand how you could be so agreeable to me, as if none of her beliefs touched you at all. So I thought Daren must have spoken to you before he died."

"What do you mean?" Jayna asked, wary.

"Whether Hasson or I took the throne, your brother would have been vizier. We both wanted him."

Shock rolled through her. "You and my brother had an alliance?"

"We were working on it," he said. "When you agreed to marry me, I was convinced he had told you about our plans." He gave a curt laugh. "You have no idea the happiness I envisioned for this marriage of ours. But you changed instantly. Once we were bound together, you let me see the truth. You hated me."

She shook her head. "I was only confused. And later, I was frightened by what Hareb and Sefu and Tiy and the others might do to us. I don't think you killed him," she said. "I did, at first, but I don't anymore."

"And you don't want me dead," he said, "though you poisoned me. It's my vizier and my closest nobles who seek my death."

The very thing Jayna feared was happening. The group had set her up to perfection. She looked guilty; they, innocent.

She fought back her rising panic. "Your poisoning was meant for me. Tiy admitted it the night Mamo was arrested—on false charges, I assure you. They know my affection for Mamo and thought to keep me quiet about their plot by threatening him." She drew a deep breath. "Tiy didn't like how close you and I seemed to be on the trip to Bene's. She found out we'd kissed that day we spent together. So she tried to poison me, as a warning. Perhaps to confine me to my bed, and away from you, until I could come to my senses."

"If this is true," he said slowly, "why didn't you tell me before now?"

At this slightest hint that he might believe her, Jayna's tension broke free in a torrent of tears. She buried her face in her hands. "I thought you would have me staked out upon the desert with my eyelids slit, that's why. I couldn't let you die, but I didn't want to die, either." Wiping her eyes, she looked at him. More tears fell across her hands as she sniffed. "I saw both our deaths in a confession. Even now, I fear you'll punish me, and they'll still get you." She'd seen it, his tomb, the writings, the dark sarcophagus. She threw her arms around him and held him tight. "You have to believe me. You have to, or you'll die!"

His arms came around her, but for only the barest touch. His hands moved to her shoulders and pried her away. "Your word could turn into their word. You understand this?"

Jayna blinked through the fog of fear that held her in its grip. Her word, their word. "Yes," she said, finally. "They'll turn everything their way. They've been doing it for days."

Amony's gaze probed deeply into her eyes. He let go of her and turned away. "Arrange one of these meetings. Let me witness one, secretly."

Jayna shook her head. "I can't."

Amony turned back to her, and his gaze narrowed.

"They don't trust me anymore," she said. "Not since—" How to bring it up, now, with his eyes so cold? "—not since I slept with you," she whispered. "They know about it. And Yera made certain to discuss it in court."

Amony gazed at her a long moment. "If I confront them, any one of them could make similar claims about you."

"They don't trust me anymore, though." He had to understand! "There's nothing I can do. I can't get in on their meetings."

"Come to me when you can."

He turned and walked away from her, back to the door.

"You're going, still?" She ran after him and caught him before he could push the portal open. "He'll kill you."

The red-brown gaze moved over face.

Jayna bit her lip. "Don't trust him."

Amony pulled away and stepped out the door.

She couldn't let it happen. The group wouldn't succeed this day. She pulled open the door Amony had exited. Both he and the young laborer were already gone. She followed the corridors that led to the rear of the palace.

Outside, a flurry of dust left its mark in the wake of the departing Pharaoh and his troop of soldiers. Jayna hurried to the barracks and stated her intention of following her husband to Sefu's estate. Though the men cautioned her about the uprising that was underway, they didn't voice their objections too loudly. Jayna got the idea that the opportunity of getting a look at the proceedings, lending a helping hand if need be, figured in their malleability toward her desires. None of the troop wanted to be anywhere but at Amony's side in case they were needed.

An excruciating half-hour later, her small force rounded the wheat fields which bordered Sefu's estate. They halted. The manicured yard was filled with tousled-looking laborers, weapons in hand, who stood still and silent.

Jayna sat, tense but relieved, to see Amony hadn't ridden into the potentially dangerous throng. He and his soldiers had stopped upon a slight incline, apart from the insurgents. He spoke, diverting the people from their anger, promising his personal intervention in the discussion of their concerns at a special forum that evening. She listened as Amony requested that they journey the short distance to the palace for food and drink and the ear of the Pharaoh. Tents would be erected to accommodate them overnight.

The stunned-looking men dispersed. They had to go to their homes and collect their wives and children who would surely want to fancy themselves up for this invitation to the palace.

Sefu rode up the hill in a chariot. Though he thought to look relieved, it was a struggle, Jayna knew. What had he planned? Had he paid one of the men within the crowd to slip a knife into Amony's back?

The two men talked a moment, then Amony shook his head and turned away.

His gaze met Jayna's across the distance.

Her heart twisted with love and pride. Did he know even a fraction of the love she felt for him?

He nodded her toward the return path home.

She turned to the guardsmen. "I guess we should go."

They turned and headed around slowly. Jayna watched, making certain that Amony safely followed them out of Sefu's territory.

Chapter Twenty-Seven

The women accepted Jayna's announcement with gravity, then frantically ordered three underlings to go into the village and solicit help. For the size of the group needing to be fed this night, they'd have to have extra hands.

Jayna retired to her chamber. Amony was back at the palace. Whatever the group had intended with the uprising at Sefu's hadn't come to pass. And now she had to devise a way to convince them that, despite her night in Amony's bed, she still supported their cause in seeing him dead. Lying back upon her cushions, she closed her eyes to think. What could she say? What could she do? She rejected one idea after another, her mind finally catching on a possibility. Coherent detail escaped her, as exhausted as she was. Holding onto the thought, she drifted off to a much needed slumber.

***

The sun was sliding ever nearer the horizon when she walked out onto the palace grounds. As Amony had promised, tents had been erected to house the people overnight. Table after table was laid out with food. A special tent with an open mouth and plenty of chairs within stood at the fore of the grounds. Here, Amony would meet with Sefu's people and discuss their grievances.

Sefu didn't look happy. Tiy stood at his side near one of the tables, her face distraught. Jayna took encouragement from the couple's seeming distress. She hoped Sefu's people would expose him for the creep he had to be. As conspirator to a killing, how kind and decent a master could he be?

Amony, flanked by his guard, as he always was in large gatherings, walked out onto the grounds. Sefu left to court the Pharaoh's side.

The hearing was about to begin.

Tiy fretted, wringing her hands. Jayna watched as the woman ate far too much from the dishes before her. Why did she appear to be on pins and needles? Because her soon-to-be husband was about to be exposed as a lousy master to his people? Did she fear that whatever set-up they'd planned for Amony might be revealed?

As the men entered the tent, and the various people scurried to get a seat, Jayna wandered close to Tiy. Sensing a presence, the woman jerked around.

The reaction pleased Jayna. Tiy was nervous, vulnerable.

"Let me back in," she said softly. "I have a plan. It'll work. Let me in, and I'll tell you about it."

"If you have a plan," Tiy snapped, "see it through." She took a large bite of honey cake as she glared at her.

Jayna kept her voice calm. "The queen is too well-known to go knocking on the villagers doors to extract the favor of killing the Pharaoh."

Sudi was the villager she spoke of—the man who raged with the slightest provocation of a simple glance, the man who'd blackened the eye of a woman who cried to hear the name *Freno*. Just before she had fallen asleep, Jayna thought of the woman and her abuser. If she could convince the group that she was trying to think up death-traps, just as they did, they might let her back in. Then she could arrange the meeting she needed to prove their guilt.

"What has this to do with the villagers?" Tiy asked.

Jayna shook her head. "I want to be a part of it. After all I've been through, I'm not going to let you get sole satisfaction. I want in on it."

Tiy eyed her with suspicion.

"Don't look at me that way," Jayna forced anger into her voice. "You may want me out of the group, but that doesn't mean I'm any less committed to the cause. So I wanted him. What of it? He has a body any woman would desire. Once." She turned her face away in momentary disgust. "I've had to play the sorrowful one when I should be laughing at him." She let a scowl curl her lips. "I want him dead, Tiy. But I need help. I want in. Talk to the others. Tell them I've got a plan."

Tiy squinted at her over the last bite of cake. "They don't trust you any more than I do. What is this plan?"

"Get me back in," Jayna said. "Then I'll tell you."

***

As a landlord, Sefu wasn't doing well. The people had one complaint after another, and each pointed to their landlord's mismanagement.   Boundaries were changed daily, most expressly in the last few days leading to the present conflict of neighbor against neighbor.   One man reaped the harvest of another's work, and lost a greater portion to yet another. Claims of yield awarded their master outweighed the set limits, yet were heartily denied by the master in question. Sefu blamed what he could on a host of underlings who had misguided him on the true state of affairs.

Tempers heated up again. After several hours of talk, the meeting concluded. Discussion would begin again on the morrow for whoever chose to remain.

Amony left the tent after the last of the men had joined their families and friends for refreshments. Jayna met him.

"Is there some entertainment we can offer?" he asked, looking over the crowd.   "A musician, or two?   Some dancing?"

She nodded. "I'll see to it."

His gaze held on her face, his eyes intent. "Is there a meeting on the agenda?"

"I'm trying," she said.

He nodded, then strolled away.

Jayna hurried off to round up the entertainment he'd requested. When the grounds were sufficiently full of music and laughter, she slipped away to visit Mamo at the jail.

Spirits had revived remarkably by the time she returned. The chance at having their grievances heard directly by the Pharaoh, combined with the festive atmosphere and flowing wine, appeared to have a beneficial effect on the laborers.

Jayna made her way through the crowd, her own guards tagging behind. She stopped a few feet short of where Amony stood watching a dance routine. Her mouth dropped open as one of the dancers, a beautiful, especially large-breasted woman did a back flip directly in front of the Pharaoh. The woman drew her gauzy red veil invitingly across her body, directing Amony's attention to her various, well-proportioned parts.

The musicians picked up a livelier tune as the dancer wiggled closer to the Pharaoh. Though Jayna took some comfort in the fact that the other dancers were doing the same thing to other guests, she watched in disbelief as the woman gyrated her flat belly beneath the king's eyes. A bright jewel twinkled from her belly button.

Amony grinned, then nodded to the man beside him. Jayna craned her neck to see who it was.

Roble.

She drew back in surprise as the man reached out and plucked the jewel away. He and Amony laughed, exchanging words she couldn't hear. The nature, though, had been very friendly. Fear prickled through her. She'd named Roble as one of Amony's enemies, so why was he laughing with the man as if they were the best of friends? Would their camaraderie deepen this night? Would Amony share with his noble the wild story she'd told him?

No. He wouldn't. He couldn't.

She stayed close all night in the hope she'd be able to talk to him, to warn him again, but the pair seemed inseparable.

Chapter Twenty-Eight

Jayna went to the kitchen to speak with the cooks and thank them for the swift, quality work they'd performed the night past. A young helper looked up from washing the countertops.

Shani. Recognition hit Jayna like a blow to the belly.

"What are you doing here?"

Her ex-lady dipped in a slight bow. "The Pharaoh hired me back as a helper."

"The Pharaoh?" Jayna echoed, dazed. "He hired you, personally?"

The woman nodded. "Yes."

Confused, angry, *hurt*, Jayna said, "Well, I'm dismissing you. Personally."

"You can't do that."

"I just did." She looked to the head cook. "The woman is dismissed."

"Your Highness?" The woman lowered her gaze and shifted nervously. "The Pharaoh told me not to dismiss the girl, except under his orders."

"Is that so?" Jayna glanced at Shani, expecting to see triumph in the woman's eyes, but there was only a quiet watchfulness. Jayna turned and marched out of the kitchen.

She located Amony in his reception chamber. He had a meeting before he rejoined the talks with the villagers. The guard admitted her to the roomful of men.

"Shani's back," she nearly hissed at the king. "In the kitchen. In this palace."

"I'm aware of that," he said, his voice low.

"You've got a lot of nerve," she said.

He didn't respond.

"Don't play with the girl's affections!"

His eyes darkened. "I don't play."

Jayna stiffened. Then looked at the men in the room beyond. This was hardly the place for a jealous scene such as the one that threatened to erupt from her.

Turning on her heel, she stormed away from him.

***

With jealousy popping through her pores, she forgot that she meant none of what she said to Tiy.

"So you see the way he humiliates me?" News of Shani's return had made the rounds quickly. "You must let me back in. If anyone hates Amony, it is I."

"We need more details," Tiy said.

"If you still have my jewels—oh, forget it. I'll supply more. There's a man in the village. His mind isn't right. He's on the edge of violence at all times. I heard his girlfriend talking about him. That's all I'm going to say. If they want to know more, and help me while I help them, they'll let me in."

Tiy's gaze traveled over her face, as if searching out the truth of her words. "I'll tell them," she said, finally.

"How is Sefu faring?" Jayna asked in an effort to appear supportive.

Tiy's gaze fell away. "He could do better."

Though it sickened her, Jayna laid her hand comfortingly on the woman's shoulder.

***

Hareb strolled up to her table during the midday meal. "We haven't had our briefing, Your Highness."

Looking up at the man, Jayna wondered if there was a warmth to his voice she'd noticed lacking these many days—even at the briefing they'd most definitely had this morning.

"Yes, you're right," she said.

"Might I suggest a stroll in the garden while we talk?"

Goosebumps rose on Jayna's arms. Had the group sent Hareb to sound her out, or to try to get her plan out of her?

As she walked out of the dining room with her chamberlain at her side, she thought fast and furiously. What could she tell him? That they'd trick Sudi into accepting her jewels somehow. Then what? Arrest him for theft? It might work. They'd lure him in front of Amony—the thought gave her chills—and supply him with a hidden knife. His sentence for thievery would drive him to violence....

Was it plausible? Would the group buy it, or at least credit her with evil intent? She had to tell Hareb part of the plan and convince him she believed in it. This was a good start, and she couldn't wreck it. She had to get herself invited to a meeting!

Chapter Twenty-Nine

Hareb remained quiet as they strolled out the doors and along the garden paths she'd trod the night she'd discovered the tomato plants. Finally, he started a light chat, and Jayna forced herself to respond. Her nerves cried out for him to get to the point. She needed to speak and see if he believed her story. She had to have the next step. The meeting. A whole-group meeting with no one left out.

The longer they walked, the more Jayna chafed. They entered the thickest part of the garden and followed the footpaths leading around the grape arbors. Still Hareb said nothing concerning the Pharaoh or the plan she'd spoken of to Tiy. They rounded the arbors, and Jayna wondered at Hareb's purpose. Why lure her out to talk, then lead her back with nothing of importance said?

The deep-green leaves that spiraled high above their heads and blocked the sun's heat certainly made for a cool reprieve, but their walk wasn't supposed to be a pleasure stroll. When would he speak of the matter so dear to her? When?

"Your Highness." He stepped aside, his arm stretched out, much in the way of that first day when he'd led her to the brink of the valley. This time, however, he directed her to a broad path leading through an archway of thick-leafed vines.

Continuing slowly past him, Jayna saw that the arbor formed a small, gazebo-like area, except, instead of being covered, a small opening let the sunshine in. A six-foot circle of sunlight fell in the center of the bricked floor at which a round stone bench stood. Of the few remaining feet outside the sunlight, half-circle benches curved on either side.

Jayna halted, still in the shadows.

Other forms disengaged from the dusk and stepped into the sunlight.

Tiy. Roble. Rana. Desta. Yera. Even Sefu!

Jayna's heart leapt. A meeting!

But Amony wasn't here!

It's okay, she thought. *Make them trust you. Get back in, and they'll arrange another that you know about ahead of time.*

She smiled. In that moment, she felt a genuine fondness for the group. She needed them, if only to expose them for who they truly were.

Keeping her smile on her face, she stepped forward into the sunlight. It was probably better this way. If Amony was listening, she'd have a hard time faking the sympathies so necessary at the moment.

She'd have to prepare herself for that next time.

If there'd be a next time.

The importance of this meeting made her quake inside.

"I have so missed you," her stress oozed from her in a sigh. She dropped her gaze to the brick floor. "You don't know how difficult it is, having no one with which to share my hatred. Nothing I've felt before rivals this. I want him dead." She looked into the faces of those who stood in the circle before her. "Am I the only one who feels destroyed, day by day, with his presence?"

Look met look, glance met glance.

"I know what you speak of."

Jayna looked at the man whose torment twisted his voice. Sefu.

Even now, Amony was in the company of Sefu's laborers, listening to the complaints against him. The man who would be king, answering to the king. Jayna fully understood the reason the group had met with her. They were desperate. Sefu was desperate.

As desperate as she.

"I'm sorry for you," she said, but for a far different reason than any of them might have supposed. "I—" the words were hard to give, but for the sake of her husband's life, she would speak them. "I grant my allegiance, now." She sank to her knees. "I consider you the rightful Pharaoh you shall soon be."

A ruffle of movement and whispers passed through the group at her words. Tiy stepped forward.

"What is your plan? We need to hear your plan."

Returning to her feet, Jayna gave her story. They agreed that the man could be used to their benefit, but questioned the details.

"I think," Jayna said, "that his anger could be directed toward Amony. If the Pharaoh questions him, it would be the Pharaoh he rages against."

"I'll have to displace the more capable guards for the day," Yera mused.

"We'd have to keep a far pace during the proceedings," Roble said.

Desta shivered. "To be sure. I wouldn't want to be nearby."

Hareb cast her a condescending look. "We need to assure that there's nothing we can do to save him."

"Oh," Desta breathed.

Roble pointed at Yera. "Anyone prone to acts of heroism will have to be seated away—"

A sudden, ear-shattering burst of vine and leaf sounded all around them. Everyone, Jayna included, spun around. Screams filled her ears. And groans. A cry escaped her own lips as her arms were yanked behind her.

Guardsmen detained every member of the group of conspirators.

Amony stepped through the paved archway. His gaze swept the secluded spot, taking in their faces. "This is a sad day," he said. "Take them."

Gazes shot Jayna's way, but seeing her similarly held, each of the group in his or her own turn looked away. Sefu twisted in his captor's grip, to no avail. Tiy bowed her head and cried as she was pushed forward. Jayna watched Amony, but his head was turned, watching as his nobles were led away.

Her heart twisted with horror as she watched the scene unfold. Then she, too, hands held behind her back, was prodded into motion—the last of the conspirators.

Amony glanced at her as the guard pushed her near.

"Halt."

The guard stopped.

Jayna stared up into her husband's hardened face.

"Release her."

He stretched his arms out to her.

A cry escaped her, and she ran to him.

He caught her against his chest and held her tight.

Chapter Thirty

The guard stepped out of the gazebo, leaving king and queen alone.

Her eyes closed, Jayna whispered near Amony's ear. "How did you know to come?"

"I've had guards reporting your every move. This looked like the opportunity we were waiting for."

"I'm sorry you had to hear all that," she moaned, thinking of the horrible things she'd said against him. "Can you forgive me? For anything?"

"I forgive you. For everything." His hold loosened, but only enough that he could look down into her eyes. "I can't blame you for wanting revenge upon the man you thought had killed your brother."

"I'm sorry I thought it was you," she said. "The truth is, by the time we were married, I didn't believe you had done it. And I never, never wanted you dead. The group began speaking of doing more than unseating you, and I didn't know how to get out, or how to tell you."

"But you did tell me."

Looking into Amony's warm eyes, Jayna felt her heart flood with emotion. "I love you."

"You love me?"

"I've always loved you," she said. "From the moment I first met you."

His gaze moved with tenderness over her face. "I've always loved you, my Queen. Always."

"Always?" she asked.

"Always and forever."

The royals returned to the palace with a private agenda. Despite a grueling day of meetings to address the conspiracy and conspirators, they concluded business before sundown.

Jayna arrived, freshly-bathed and swathed in her new golden robe, at Amony's chamber. The Pharaoh, refreshed as she, and looking as full of anticipation, pulled her into his arms.

"We share this chamber, now. Let this be the last time you need to make a special journey to be in my arms."

Jayna chuckled at his choice of words. "Any journey is worth the effort as long as I end up here."

She caressed his stalwart chest, letting her questing palms glide over his shoulders.

His hands moved, too, kneading sensual waves of pleasure across her back. "You'll move your belongings in?"

She smiled into his passion-warmed eyes. "Of course. As soon as you'd like."

"Morning will be soon enough," he said, and his lips claimed hers.

***

"I have an apology of my own."

"An apology?" Jayna murmured, her mind and body still languid from passionate lovemaking. She raised her head out of the crook of her husband's cradling shoulder, and peered up at him.

"I doubted you about the poison."

"Oh, that," she breathed, remembering the pain of his distrust.

"I'll never doubt you again."

"Never?" she asked.

"Never." He rolled over, trapping her in the heavenly center of his firm chest and muscular arms. "You can tell me the sky is full of crocodiles, and the river full of stars, and I'll believe you."

A smile tugged at the corner of her mouth. "Interesting that you should exaggerate so."

"I'm not exaggerating," he said, his red-brown eyes intense. "It's a measure of how much I love you, and trust you. I'll always believe you. From this moment on, I'll never doubt you. Do you believe me?" he asked, his eyes searching hers. "I hate that I doubted you. I hate all the doubts I've harbored."

"Me, too," Jayna said.

Her husband's lips met hers in a long, deep kiss.

Jayna ran her hands over his thick, silky shoulders, into his soft hair. They kissed, their hands and mouths touching, exploring. No longer did anything stand in their way. King and Queen were free to love. No doubts edged in upon their solitude. Jayna hadn't even the queen to contend with. She and the queen were one and the same—and at peace. The wretched future she'd been allowed to see had been averted. She and Amony would live. And love.

Darkness descended. The royals lit a lotus bloom oil lamp near the bed. A gentle yellow glow fell over the golden sheet and the couple who lay entwined. Cozy, their voices soft, they spoke of little things until Jayna brought up what rested most in her mind. "That thing you said—about believing me—?"

"No little thing, trust." Her husband's arm tightened around her. "It's everything."

"I agree." Jayna drew a deep breath. "But, would you believe me even if I told you I came back to you from the future? Four-thousand years to be exact."

Amony chuckled. "You were born twenty-some years ago, there's no disputing that."

"I was," Jayna said softly, carefully, treading a path she had trouble understanding herself. "And then I was born later."

A slow smile crept over Amony's mouth.

Seeing it, Jayna twisted in his arms and raised up on his chest to better look at him. "I was," she said. "I was born four-thousand years from now. I saw your tomb."

She told him all of it, alternately stunning him, confusing him, *convincing* him.

"The worst part," she said at last, "was believing I'd killed you. I thought, from what the tomb said and showed, from what it seemed the moment the brick fell, that you died by your wife's hands. My hands."

He shook his head, his fingers moving softly over her back. "What happened to you?" he asked quietly. "In the tomb?"

Frowning, Jayna bit the inside of her lip. "I don't know."

"If you have a life in the future, will you return to it?" Her husband's hands flattened against her, drawing her tightly to him. "If—" His brows drew together, and he stared at her in furious concentration. "Am I to lose a part of you one day and not even know it?"

Jayna searched her husband's eyes. "I don't think so. I hope not. It feels so right here. I feel so right. I can't imagine leaving where I belong." She smiled. "Do you know what I did in that other life?"

"What?" he asked.

"I studied you," she said. "Egyptians. Great Pharaohs. I think a part of me knew all along and was guiding me so I could come back to you."

"I'm glad you came to my tomb to get lost. What if you'd stumbled upon any other Pharaoh? Some other man would have you right now."

She smiled at his play. "I was meant to go to your tomb. I was meant for you."

"You were," he agreed. "And you must stay."

"Don't let me go," she said.

"Never." His eyes blazing with love and tenderness, he pulled her into both his arms and against his heart.

Jayna kissed him, then drew back. Passion flared anew. Amony pressed her back upon the sheet and buried his face in her neck.

Chapter Thirty-One

Sticky, wet blood streamed past her fingertips.

"No!" The cry tore from her.

She jerked upright.

Amony was dead, a knife in his back.

She'd killed him. The writings in the tomb had come true. The green-eyed queen had killed her husband.

Jayna had killed him.

Strong arms cradled her. "What is it? What's wrong?"

Sweat poured down her face. The sheets were damp, and she shook with fear.

She'd killed Amony.

But it was just a dream. He was alive.

He was alive!

She threw her arms around him and held him tight. His arms encircled her, his voice soft as he crooned, "It's all right. It's all right...."

She pulled away. "But it's not." Looking into her husband's loving, trusting face, she felt true horror course through her blood. "You're not safe." She leaped from the bed, her chest heaving with the effort of breathing. "You can't be alone with me."

"We've arrested them," Amony said.

Jayna shook her head. "All along, I've believed that I killed you. Don't you understand? Something happens. As long as I'm here with you, you're not safe."

Amony got out of bed and came around to her. "Where would you go?"

"I don't know." She stumbled away from him. "I don't know what I'm feeling, what I'm doing, or thinking, but something isn't right. Oh Amony, I'm so afraid!"

He caught her arm and pulled her gently against him. "You don't honestly think you'll hurt me, do you?"

"I don't know," she cried. "I just feel, all of a sudden, oh—who am I to change the past? How do I know that any of what I've done or felt has made a difference? What if I'm wrong? What if the Jayna you married is lying dormant? What if she does hurt you? You know, the night you were poisoned—I'm so sorry—I didn't hear you. Atep said you would have felt a lot of pain. I don't remember hearing a thing. What if I'm wrong, and these memories and feelings I've been having are...false? What if I've fooled myself, and fooled you, and she is a killer? What if I am a killer?"

Amony gripped her arms. "I've known you from the beginning. You've been angry and mysterious and confused, but you've never been evil. You've tried to hurt me—yes. But by disobeying me. By flouting my command. By being a kind, beautiful woman with a secret grudge that, by its very nature, I had no idea how to overcome. You've hurt me by denying me your love. I've never witnessed you hurting anyone else, in any way. It's not in you."

Her heart swelled at his words. "I love you," she said. "And I'm afraid you're going to die. I want you to live."

"I'm alive."

Jayna laughed. "That's what you first said to me—"

A blast tore through her ribs, as if an enormous fist had slammed into her chest. She flung out a hand, and Amony caught her from crashing to the floor.

"Jayna!" he cried hoarsely.

She could barely draw a breath as she looked into his eyes. Her heart tripped to see the shock on his face.

"That was strange, wasn't it?" she panted.

Tears sprang to her eyes. Tears of pain, and fear. Nothing had caused the blow, nothing she could see, yet it had come from outside her.

The connecting reception room door opened slightly.

She glanced beyond Amony, and he turned. She expected to see a guard step into the room, though such an intrusion would have been highly improper.

The nobleman, Nassor, appeared to have no such qualms.

Both Jayna and Amony stared at the man in stunned disbelief.

A smile curled the corner of Nassor's mouth as he observed, "The royal couple doesn't sleep. Your foes are gone—almost, anyway." His gaze settled on Jayna who held a hand clutched to her chest. "I'm ashamed of you, my Queen. I thought you, at least, would never assume life should go so easy." He paced near. "I paid attention at our little talks. Didn't you?" He smiled, then adopted a false frown. "I guess not. If you had, you wouldn't be surprised by this."

Jayna realized his smile was false, his frown real, as he pulled a knife from his kilt. *Her knife*, the jewel-studded dagger that usually rested at the bottom of her clothes chest.

"It's my guess that you're surprised," he said.

Jayna opened her mouth to speak, but the horrific pain slammed through her chest again. Before Nassor's surprised gaze, she stumbled backward. Her legs gave out beneath her, and she felt Amony's arms wrap around her, guiding her to the floor.

She wanted to cry out to him, tell him of her fear, but her head jerked back as though a physical presence shoved at her, and blackness sapped her vision.

A firm body pressed against hers. Amony's. She felt him, but couldn't see him. As if from far away, she heard him calling to her. He said more, but she couldn't make out the words.

A mouth closed over hers.

It wasn't Amony's. These lips were different, and they forced wind into her lungs that she didn't need. She was full. She turned her head and twisted against the hands that pawed her in the darkness.

Strong arms tightened around her.

A shout sounded in her ears.

The blackness fell away for a split second, and she saw Nassor in the dim, yellow light, a dagger—her dagger—raised high, the point arching down toward Amony.

She tried to scream but the voices echoed around her, drowning her out...

'Breathe, breathe, breathe!'

Amony left her. He twisted away, separating their warm bodies.

The cold seized her.

'Breathe! Breathe!'

"Amony!" she cried out for him. He had to come back. The cold was taking her. "Amony!"

Chapter Thirty-Two

"Look at this."

The deep sigh sounded loud, now that the cacophony of voices and shouts had quieted within the dank tomb.

Four pairs of eyes gazed at the walls.

"It's beautiful."

"Yeah." Another sigh sounded. "This guy had it all."

"And she found him."

Gazes moved to the woman who lay lifeless on the floor of the tomb. They'd reached her too late. Their attempts at CPR had proved futile.

"She'll get credit for it," another assured.

The gazes returned to the drawings that surrounded them. The handsome king and his green-eyed queen were pictured everywhere—seated on their royal chairs, holding hands beside the River Nile. Cradling a tiny infant.

Chapter Thirty-Three

Jayna looked around the grounds. Tents had been erected again, tables laid out with food and refreshments. People milled about, talking and laughing. Servants brought torches out to light the waning evening. The conspirators could harm them no longer, not even Sefu, who'd confessed to the murders of both Daren and Hasson. The new appointments to Amony's court had been made, and this reception would celebrate them all.

Amony slipped his arm around Jayna's shoulders, surprising her.

"Where did you come from?" she asked.

"Where did you?" he teased.

She smiled. "The important thing to know is where I am." She snuggled against his firm torso. "How's your arm?"

He twisted his forearm for her inspection.

"Your bandage is gone," she observed. "Atep removed it?"

"No. He coddles me. I did it."

"Are you sure it was time?"

"Looks good, doesn't it?"

She frowned at the long gash. It didn't look very good to her at all, but it was much, much better an injury than he might have sustained. Nassor had only managed to slice Amony's arm, rather than embed the knife in his back before the guards rushed in from the lavatory. Jayna smiled, thinking of those big, fierce men hiding away the night huddled around the toilet.

She'd been unconscious for several hours before she learned that Amony, sensing an ulterior plot in her futuristic accounting of his death, had waited until she slept, then quietly summoned the handful of guards to watch over them in their slumber. He intended to have a constant, secret guard until no threat revealed itself to them.

She looked up at her husband and smiled. All thoughts of an evil Queen and a dead Pharaoh were behind her.

Amony was alive.

And she was here.

She had earned the trust of the man she loved. The four-thousand-year-old betrayal had been rectified.

Her husband gazed down at her through warm, loving eyes. He pulled her to him. "I love you."

His head dipped, and she closed her eyes on the sight of sweet, boyish freckles dotting a majestic face before he kissed her, sweeping her with him to the place of man and woman and ecstasy.

ABOUT THE AUTHOR

Dimitri Eann resides in Michigan with her Virginia-born husband and four children. Outside of her busy schedule, she enjoys writing as well as curling up with a good book.

Dimitri would love to hear from you. You may write to her in care of ImaJinn Books, or email her at DimitriEan@aol.com